LIFE in the GRAND PAUSE

ISBN 978-1-946425-36-2 Softcover
ISBN 978-1-946425-38-6 Hardcover
Library of Congress Control Number: 2019935024

Book Design by CSinclaire Write-Design
Cover Art by David Martinez

• BARNSLEY INK •
RALEIGH, NORTH CAROLINA
a Write Way Publishing Company imprint

• Books by Frank Saraco •

Hugo's Dilemma
The Bald and the Beautiful
It Could Have Been Us
The Ninth Street Mystery

Dedicated to my mother,
Maria Saraco.

She applauds my inspiration,
challenges my limitations,
and is a constant source of strength.

What Readers Are Saying ...

"Sometimes it takes a life-changing event to show us what is most important. Through the eyes of a ten year old boy, Frank Saraco explores the intricacies of empathy, acceptance, and most importantly kindness—which he shows must be extended even to those who are not kind to us in return. In teaching us this crucial lesson, *Life in the Grand Pause* is an act of kindness in itself."

— **Melissa Loflin, Media Specialist**

"This book has a lot of random acts of kindness or RAK as [students] call them. This is an inspiring and uplifting book that has many twists and turns."

— **Lindsay B., 6th grader, LMS**

LIFE in the GRAND PAUSE

a middle-grade novel

Frank Saraco

• BARNSLEY INK •
RALEIGH, NORTH CAROLINA

CONTENTS

EARLY SPRING, PRESENT DAY

A CACOPHONY OF SOUNDS could be heard from off-stage as the early arrivals began warming up. The green room, located back-stage adjacent to a row of dressing rooms, was bustling with chatter, last-minute wardrobe adjustments, and the clanking of instrument cases. Many of the featured musicians had their own dressing room, but Preston bypassed his and entered the green room carrying his Man Claudiu cello inside a sturdy but slightly worn case. The cello was an elite, handmade, $16,000 gem from Northern Italy, but Preston, being very down-to-earth and at least ten years

1

younger than the next youngest of his orchestra peers, never bragged or called attention to this treasure. Passing the large mirror, Preston put down his case and adjusted his bow tie and vest before putting on his tailcoat. A tall, dark-haired musician entered the room just as Preston took one last glance in the mirror to adjust a lock of blonde hair that had fallen out of place. Spying Josh in the mirror's reflection, he turned and extended his hand.

"Hey, Josh! I was glad to see your name on the list," Preston said.

"Yeah, you get to play with the best!" Josh jested. "I'm glad you could make it for the performance."

"I tried to get here for the final rehearsal, but my soccer team made it to the spring tournament, and I couldn't let my teammates down. We took first place, so I was definitely thrilled to be there. The conductor and I spoke on FaceTime last night. I'm sure he covered all the necessary details for tonight."

"He's the best around and has been looking forward to having you perform. And congrats on the soccer win!" Josh said while laying down his case. "Why aren't you in your dressing room?"

"I really don't need a dressing room. Besides, it's too quiet and lonely."

"I've always said they give those dressing rooms to the wrong people! Just kidding! Well … maybe!" Josh laughed at his wisecrack. "Hey, I've got a brilliant idea. Why don't we store our cases there? The packing up will be much easier."

"Okay, give me a second to pull out my cello and bow." Preston opened his case and carefully lifted out the cello by its neck. He grabbed the bow and tucked it under his arm, then closed his case and handed it to Josh.

"I'll be back in a few." Josh was almost out the door when Preston noticed a smudge on his cello.

"Hey, Josh! When you're in the dressing room, grab the polishing cloth from my case, if you don't mind. I just spotted a smudge on the side panel."

"Sure!" Josh answered back above the growing clatter. "Where do you think it is?"

"It's either in the outside pocket or inside the case."

"Got it! By the way, thanks for letting my case hang out with yours," Josh joked and walked quickly toward the dressing room trying to balance the empty case in his left hand while carrying his full case with his right.

Josh placed both cases on the dressing room floor. He took his cello and bow from his case and carefully leaned them against the wall. "Polishing cloth," Josh muttered. He checked the side compartment of Preston's case. He felt something and pulled it out. It was a folded piece of paper.

Josh automatically unfolded the paper to see what it was. It was a simple message in neat cursive.

Break a leg, R.J.!
Sincerely, Ella

Thinking it was an odd note, Josh tucked it in his pocket and continued to look for the polishing cloth. He eventually found it tidily folded in a small compartment inside the case. Josh added the cloth to the same pocket as the note, grabbed his cello and bow, and headed to the stage. He handed Preston the polishing cloth on the way to his seat.

"I also found this note in the outside pocket and ..." Josh hesitated for a second before continuing, "sorry, but I read it without thinking. Before you get mad, it doesn't even belong to you."

"Huh?"

"It's for some guy named R.J. I bet his girlfriend put it in the wrong case."

"Wait, let me see it." Preston opened the note Josh handed him, read the words, and smiled.

"Do you know R.J.?"

"Wow, I haven't heard that name in six years."

"Who is it?" Josh was intrigued by the mystery.

"It's a long story."

"Okay, so go on." Josh was hooked.

"Let's pick up this conversation after the concert."

"You're killing me, Preston."

"I told you, it's a long story. Besides, the stage manager just walked in, and we're out of time."

"You're off the hook for now. But you are not going to any after parties! We have a late dinner meeting back at your favorite New York all-night diner." Josh gave Preston a look that said *you better keep your promise* before grabbing his bow and beginning his warm up.

The Metropolitan Opera House never disappointed, and the audience was standing and applauding within milliseconds of the last note. It was a performance for the books, and as expected, Preston was phenomenal. He stepped forward when directed by the conductor and took his bow. The audience's applause grew even louder. Preston began acknowledging the orchestra and then the director. Thoughts of his conversation with Josh were swirling in his head, and his smile broadened as he fondly remembered R.J. Looking back at the orchestra he spotted Josh, who was sporting the *you're not getting out of telling me* look. He gave Josh a half nod and then sat down and poised his bow to play an encore. Instantly, the audience became silent and mesmerized as they listened to the artistry of a true musical genius.

Later that evening

"I'll let you take a few bites before you fill me in on all the details," Josh said, grabbing one of Preston's fries.

"Do you want an abridged version or the whole story?"

"This place is open twenty-four hours, and I told your parents I'd make sure you got back to their hotel safely. I want the whole story," Josh said around a huge bite of his pastrami sandwich.

"Okay, you asked for it. I'll tell you the full story of R.J., but I need to take you back to my fifth grade year. Let's see ... here's how it all went ..." Preston took another bite of his sandwich and allowed his memories to flood his mind. It was going to be a long night, but it was time to remember R.J. and the students at Fern Creek Elementary.

CHAPTER ONE

FIRST DAY, NEW SCHOOL

THE LATE BELL RANG as Mom completed the last of the registration forms in the school office. After she handed them to the friendly lady behind the counter, we were directed to have a seat. As I looked around, I knew immediately that the school had recently undergone some renovations. Earlier, as we stood outside the front office waiting to be buzzed in, I noticed a bronze plaque prominently displayed by the front entrance. It read, "Fern Creek Elementary established 1962." I could recognize the familiar but faint fumes of fresh paint and new carpet. Whoever was in charge of the remodel seemed to know how to mash-up the original with the new. Mom was handling the urge to inspect the work rather well, which surprised me.

It is good having Mom sit beside me, especially after the events of the last few days. Looking at her from the corner of my eye, I couldn't help but shake my head. She looked so different. I mean, I still knew it was her, but I don't think most of her friends would recognize her. I don't think my *grandma* would recognize her! Her hair is short and very blonde. She is wearing horn-rimmed glasses and simple earrings. And her clothes, well, let's say they are a total one-eighty from her usual style. She is definitely acting different too. A faint smile appeared on Mom's face as a woman walked toward us. Wearing a warm, friendly smile, the lady stuck out her hand in Mom's direction as we stood up.

"Good morning, Mrs. Baker! My name is Mrs. Grant. I'm the principal of Fern Creek Elementary," she said, shaking Mom's hand. She then looked in my direction.

"Richard," she said and then asked, "is that what you would like to be called?"

"Well, ma'am ..." I started then looked to Mom for help.

"He likes to go by R.J.," Mom said. I nodded my head in agreement.

"Well then, R.J. it is! We are excited to have you at Fern Creek Elementary. This year we will celebrate our fiftieth anniversary. Up until a few weeks ago, this office and most of the school was covered in dust from our renovation project."

"That's hard to believe," Mom interjected. "It looks so clean."

"Thank you. Our custodians and many of our students' parents helped with the clean up over spring break. R.J., I thought I'd walk you to your new class. You will be in Mr. Bailey's class. He's an exceptional teacher, and I know you will enjoy the last few months of fifth grade with him."

"I'm sure he will," Mom said, grabbing her purse beside the chair.

"Aren't you coming with us?" I asked.

"Honey, I need to attend a job orientation this morning. Remember, we talked about this last night. It starts at 8:30, and I don't want to be late."

"Don't worry, R.J. Your mom can see your classroom on another day."

"I'll see you after school. I plan to make

your favorites for dinner." Mom handed me lunch money and hurried away to her orientation.

I looked at Mrs. Grant, and before I knew it, we were walking down the main hallway on our way to the fifth grade wing. Walking past the glass-doored displays, I caught a glimpse of my image in the reflection. I stopped in my tracks. Who was that? I didn't recognize him at all. Sure, inside I felt the same, well ... sort of, I guess. I didn't know that boy with brown hair and brown eyes who stared back at me. Definitely not the way anyone would have described me three days ago. Who was this impostor that used to be me? Suddenly, I was startled back to reality by the hug of a young girl.

"Thank you for welcoming our new student, Natalia. Now it's time for you to get back to class and back to learning!" Mrs. Grant said, smiling at both of us.

"Okay, Mrs. Grant," the little girl said, staring at me the whole time. After giving me a big smile, she skipped back to her classroom.

"Please walk, Natalia," ordered Mrs. Grant in a quiet, calm voice.

"Yes, ma'am."

Mrs. Grant said, "She is an amiable girl,

but I've never seen her hug an unfamiliar student before. Do you know her?"

"No, ma'am. We just moved here. I've never seen her before," I answered, trying to shake off a feeling of déjà vu.

"Hmm. She probably could tell that you needed a hug right about now. Starting a new school in a new town this late in the school year is not easy," she said as we continued to walk. We made a left turn and entered a landing with stairs. As we walked up the stairs, I noticed a quote at the top of the stairway that read "You are not better than anyone, but no one is better than you." I repeated it several times in my mind as we made our way down the hall. An assortment of artwork and student projects was displayed neatly on both sides of this hall. You could tell that it was fifth grade work. As we approached Mr. Bailey's room, I saw there was a quote above his door. This one read, "The only thing we have to fear is fear itself." — Franklin D. Roosevelt.

"Yeah, right!" I didn't mean to say it out loud, but there it was. No taking it back now.

"Is something wrong, R.J.?" Mrs. Grant asked.

"No, not all!" I had to think quickly. "I ... I

was ... thinking about a bet my sister made with me last night. She bet that her school would be better than mine."

"Where does she go to school?"

"We dropped her off at Forest Ridge High School before coming here this morning."

"Forest Ridge *is* a pretty amazing school."

"Fern Creek seems way better to me!"

"Glad you think so," Mrs. Grant said, smiling.

Whew, that was a close call. I thought I was pretty convincing. Honestly, for a second, I believed it myself. I was told this would get easier, but I don't know. We entered the room. For a classroom, it was totally cool. Students sat at tables, and each table had one of those professional nameplates with a team name displayed. Mr. Bailey was working at a small table with a handful of students. He looked up and spotted Mrs. Grant and quickly came over to us.

"Mr. Bailey, this is R.J. Baker, your new student."

"R.J., glad to meet you! Welcome to Team Bailey!" Mr. Bailey looked to be about the same age as my uncle. He was sporting some Chucks and a bow tie. An interesting combination, but it seemed to work for him.

"Thank you," I said as eyes now stared through me. I felt my face turn red, but Mr. Bailey seemed to know the right words to say.

"Boys and girls, this is R.J. Baker. He was new about a minute ago, but now he just made us boys thirteen and girls twelve! Boys, we're officially the majority!"

A girl called out from the back of the room, "That's only because you included yourself in the total, Mr. Bailey!"

"Yeah, you don't count!" another girl chimed.

"Now, now—let's not get stuck in the technicalities," Mr. Bailey said, grinning as he put out a fist bump. I obliged. "Now, let's get back to work. Thank you, Mrs. Grant, for making my day!"

"R.J., you're in good hands. I'm off to a meeting."

"Thank you, Mrs. Grant," I said, still feeling unsure about all this.

Mr. Bailey walked me over to my table and then asked Andy, a short boy with glasses, to show me around the room and help me find my cubby. I was now part of the Trail Blazers, the team name of my table. Andy, along with two girls, Jennilee and Sophie, were the other teammates. This whole teammate setup was different from my other school, but I won't go there at the moment.

"Hey, R.J.," Sophie whispered during guided reading, "are you any good at kickball?"

"Kickball?" I whispered back, wondering why she decided to ask that particular question at this very moment.

"Yeah, we'll fill you in at lunch. Mr. Bailey isn't keen on off-task behavior during our reading block. He takes reading very seriously. Come to think of it, he takes kickball pretty seriously, too."

I gave her a half-hearted smile as I was still not sure what she meant. After scanning the written directions on the board, I grabbed a book from the back counter and began reading chapter one in *Mr. Popper's Penguins*. I'd never read it before, but I had seen the movie, which was pretty funny. Hopefully, the book would be just as good.

CHAPTER TWO

MATHEMATICS

I MANAGED TO GET through the first eight chapters of *Mr. Popper's Penguins* before the reading block was finished. The book was actually pretty good. I smiled when I read the part about Captain Cook gathering odd items from around the house to build a nest in the refrigerator. It reminded me of the time I tried to see if the refrigerator light stayed on when the door was closed. Not my brightest hour, but still a memory that my family brings up when they find the need to, as Dad puts it, "keep me humble."

So far Mr. Bailey seemed like an awesome teacher. Since I never had a male teacher before, I wasn't sure what to expect. Everyone knew exactly what to do each time a chime played. It was pretty impressive. I don't think it took more than twenty seconds for everyone to move, pull out their materials, and get settled. Luckily, my teammates helped me with each transition, so I didn't feel overwhelmed.

"Let me get you a whiteboard," Andy said as everyone else turned to read the math problem of the day.

"Thanks," I said. Andy went to the back cupboard and pulled out a new whiteboard, a blue Expo marker, and a white sock from the drawer beside the sink.

"Here you go. I thought you might like a blue Expo," he said, handing me the items.

"Yeah, I do. How did you know?"

"I really didn't. It's all Mr. Bailey has left," Andy said half laughing.

Mr. Bailey projected a word problem on the flat screen TV, and everyone began to read it quietly. In an instant, they were all writing on their whiteboards, so I did the same. One by one students started standing and waiting for their teammates to do the same. I knew this routine. It was called Numbered Heads Together. Once everyone at the table was up on their feet, each person presented his or her answer. Jennilee went first at our table.

"My answer is thirty three-ninths or three and two thirds."

"I have the same," Sophie stated showing her board.

"I have three and six ninths," Andy shared.

"That's the same answer, Andy," I said, showing how I simplified the fraction.

"Oh, I forgot to do that," Andy said, looking down at his board.

"So, do we all agree?" Jennilee asked.

"Yes," we all said in unison and sat down.

Mr. Bailey was circulating, listening to groups discussing their answers and reaching a consensus. He smiled and held up his thumb when he listened to our group. When everyone was seated, Mr. Bailey pulled out a card from a box, glanced at it, and said, "It looks like the Trail Blazers will be sharing their answer and work today. Any volunteers?" The team immediately looked at me. I wasn't ready to do this, but Mr. Bailey didn't waste one minute.

"Okay, R.J., it looks like your teammates have selected you. Please come up to the whiteboard and talk us through how you solved the problem."

Immediately, the class began to clap. I hadn't done anything yet, and they were already applauding. Apparently, it was a way to encourage participation. I guess it worked because I found my way to the board, picked up the red Expo marker, and began explaining my strategy for solving the problem. It wasn't that bad. For a moment I completely forgot that I was the new guy. Maybe I *could* do this.

CHAPTER THREE

LUNCHTIME

THE MORNING MOVED ALONG quickly. When it was 11:25, Mr. Bailey walked over to the classroom door, and everyone stood up. He scrunched his face like he was thinking really hard and then said, "Reverse."

The students one by one began to line up, some grabbing lunch boxes from the cubbies. There was some kind of order to this line-up, most likely alphabetical order in reverse, and I really wasn't sure when it would be my turn. Sophie grabbed my arm and said, "You're behind me. I'm Beekman, you're Baker."

"Thanks," I said, following behind her.

So far everyone seemed friendly. Well, at least my teammates were all great.

Walking to the lunchroom, we passed a few other classes heading to specials or recess. A few students waved to me, and others just stared. Up until now, I had never felt like a stranger at school. Today, I felt like a stranger in more ways than I cared to acknowledge.

The cafeteria smelled like my old cafeteria. The cafeteria ladies were all friendly, and they made me feel welcome.

"Did you want any extras today?" the cashier asked when I reached the end of the serving line.

"Extras?" I repeated, not sure what she meant.

"On Mondays, you have a choice of a fruit bar or yogurt with granola," she clarified. "If you decide you would like an extra, I will give you a purple ticket, which you will present to the lady behind the cart after you finish your main entry."

"No, I'll pass for today," I said, not sure that I had enough money.

Andy, Sophie, and Jennilee were waiting for me to finish before leading me to our table.

"Thanks for waiting up for me," I said.

"Sure, that's what teammates do," Andy said. "And besides, I'm glad to have another boy in our group."

"We are allowed to talk as long as we keep the volume down," Sophie said as she opened her lunch box. She pulled out a turkey and cheese sandwich and some apple slices. I ate a tater tot before taking a big bite of a grilled cheese sandwich that smelled delicious.

"So, are you good at kickball?" Sophie asked just as I took that bite.

"Kickball?" I asked trying to cover my mouth that was now full of warm, melted cheese and toasted bread.

"Yeah, kickball. Each year, the fifth grade classes have a huge kickball competition the second week of May. Mr. Bailey's class has had two consecutive wins. We are hoping to make it win number three this year."

Andy added, "We practice every other day at recess."

"When is recess?" I asked.

"Right after lunch and today we have the field," Jennilee answered.

"Do you have a preferred position?" Andy asked.

"I'm not sure," I answered reluctantly.

"Well, you can take right field until we find the best spot for you. Sophie is at third base, and Jennilee is just behind second base."

"I think I'll just watch today," I said.

"We're only weeks away from the tournament, so you need to get in the game today," Sophie said before taking the last bite of her sandwich.

"Are you sure I can't just watch for today?" I asked, hoping to convince them to let me sit out.

"You're part of Team Bailey, and we can't miss one practice. It's bad enough when we lose a practice to rain. Mr. Bailey is very competitive. Last week it began pouring before Mr. Bailey had us quit and run inside. He's determined to keep the trophy another year," Andy explained.

"On Friday, he told the class that he's grown quite fond of that old trophy and would probably cry all summer if it ever left the shelf behind his desk," Jennilee said.

"I'm sure he's exaggerating," I said.

"No, you should have seen him when we almost lost the Multiplication Fact Round-off against the other fifth grade classes earlier this year. Luckily, we pulled ahead during the last round. I'm telling you, he's totally obsessed with winning! You would never suspect that just looking at him. I can't imagine letting him down," said Andy.

"Couldn't I be the scorekeeper? I just got here, and it probably wouldn't be fair for me to compete as I haven't been part of the class the whole year." I was hoping to find some loophole, but the odds didn't seem to be in my favor.

CHAPTER FOUR

RECESS

"OKAY, R.J. CAN BE on your team for today's practice," Thomas said pointing to Jennilee, Sophie, Andy, and an assortment of students whose names I hadn't memorized yet.

"I can just watch today if that makes it easier." I tried one last time, but my attempt was pointless. Andy and Thomas walked toward the center of the group, and Sophie handed Andy a coin.

"I call *heads*," said Thomas.

"*Tails*," added Andy.

Thomas tossed the coin in the air, caught it in his hand, and slammed it into his open palm. "Tails!" Thomas announced, handing the coin back to Sophie.

"Here's the kicking order—Jennilee, Blake, Emma, Robby, Zoe, R.J., Scarlett, Spencer, Olivia, me, Sophie, and Trey," Andy called out as we headed toward the fence.

"I can go last," I suggested hoping that recess would end before it was my turn.

"No, not necessary," Andy said, patting me on the back.

"Let's do this!" Jennilee shouted, heading to the plate.

It looked like Thomas was going to be the pitcher for the other team. He walked over to the center and bounced the ball as he scanned the field. His teammates each took their place on the field and within seconds the ball came rolling toward Jennilee. She started running toward home plate as the ball passed the half-way point. When her foot made contact with the ball, I could hear the impact echo behind me.

Jennilee was good. She made it to third base just like that. Looking toward home plate, I could see Blake getting ready to kick. Mr. Bailey was standing halfway between third base and home plate. His arms were crossed, and he nodded his head and winked at Jennilee as she looked over his way.

I could see that this was serious, and my heart started pounding even harder. Looking around the large playground, I saw two other classes practicing on other corners of the expansive field. Their teachers were right there with them. It seemed funny to me to see one of them wearing a girly dress with Converse sneakers. My sister always called dresses with flowing bits "girly" dresses. I found the whole scene quite funny, but no one else seemed to think so.

I spotted Robby running toward the oncoming ball. He only made a base hit. I guess that's what you call it in kickball. I'm not really sure. As Zoe prepared for her turn, she looked at me and smiled. "You're next, R.J.!" she yelled as she sprinted to take her place. My mouth became dry, and I could feel my body break out in a cold sweat. I saw Mr. Bailey pull out a whistle. Come on and blow your whistle, Mr. Bailey. Let recess be over. He blew the whistle, but recess wasn't over.

"You're out Robby and Zoe!" he exclaimed.

Zoe had hit a fly ball, and some kid in

the center field caught it and tagged out Robby before he made it safely back to first base.

"You're up, R.J.!" Andy yelled, trying to be heard over the outfield's loud cheers. I felt sick. It was worse than having the flu. I can't do this. Why can't I just sit out?

"R.J.! R.J.! R.J.!" the class began to chant. This wasn't helping. All eyes were on me, and for the first time in a very long time, I felt inadequate—like a nothing. I sprinted toward the base. By now, my entire back was drenched, and my head was spinning. I watched as Thomas pulled the ball back and lunged it toward me. It was time for me to run. My head began throbbing as I ran, and then it all went black.

CHAPTER FIVE

THE AFTERMATH

I COULD SEE FAINT glimpses of blue sky as
I slowly opened my eyes.

"R.J., are you okay?" Mr. Bailey was hov-
ering over me holding a bottle of water. "I think
you're dehydrated. Did you have anything to
drink for lunch?"

"Huh, who? What?" Suddenly, I realized
what I was saying and tried to think of something that could explain the confusion. "Sorry,
Mr. Bailey, I think you're right about the dehy-
dration." Mr. Bailey seemed to believe me and
offered me a hand up. I still felt light-headed
once I stood up, so Mr. Bailey walked me over

to the benches. I sat down, hoping this would all go away. Everyone started crowding around me, making it harder to get past the events of the last few minutes.

"Andy and Jennilee, please take R.J. to the nurse's office."

"Sure thing, Mr. Bailey," Andy responded, walking over to my side. As we walked across the field, I could hear a few students laughing. They were laughing at me. I knew it and so did Andy and Jennilee. They just shook their heads in disappointment.

"Don't even give that a second thought, R.J. They're just a bunch of immature ten- or eleven-year-olds," Jennilee said as we entered the building.

"They're Mrs. Granger's students and not a very good example of what it takes to be a Fern Creek Sparrow," Andy added.

"What does it take to be a Fern Creek Sparrow?" I asked.

"It takes perseverance, respectfulness, integrity, and kindness. Our class has almost earned the RAK Award," explained Jennilee.

"The rack award? What's that?" I asked.

"R A K. It stands for 'Random Acts of Kindness.' Almost every student in our class has posted a RAK experience on Mr. Bailey's class website. We're so close." Andy turned down a short hallway and led us to a small room. "Here's the nurse's office. Nurse Mitchell is the best around. We'll see you back in class," he said with a wave.

"Why thank you, Andrew Mitchell," she called after them. Turning to me she said, "You must be R.J."

"Wow, you are good," I said.

"Yes, I'm good at my job, but I didn't know your name until your teacher called me on the walkie-talkie to tell me you were on your way from the field."

"Oh," I said.

She waved me to a chair beside her desk. "How are you feeling now?" she asked.

"My head is still spinning," I answered.

"It appears that you hit the ground hard when you fainted. It's not that warm yet, but I can see that your shirt is drenched. Is anything else bothering you?" she asked.

Now that was a loaded question if I ever heard one, but I knew the only thing I could say would be a lie. "No. I'm just tired from all the moving, that's all." Lying was becoming more natural, which isn't something I feel should merit bragging rights.

"Why don't you sip on some cold orange juice," she suggested as she opened the small fridge beside the counter, "and then rest on the recovery couch for a few minutes.

After a few sips of juice, I stretched out and closed my eyes, hoping to calm myself, but thoughts about the last few days flooded my mind, and for once in my life, I wished I could just disappear.

CHAPTER SIX

ONE DAY EARLIER — APRIL 15TH

MY NAME IS RICHARD. Richard Baker. Richard James Baker. I was born July twelfth, no twenty-first. My sister's name is Mallory. Why can't I remember her middle name? Mallory Christine? No. Mallory Kirs ... Kirsten. Yeah, that's it. Mallory Kirsten Baker. My mom, Candice Baker. Candy Baker, what were they thinking? My dad, Philip James Baker.

Oh, I get the connection. Dad and I now have the same middle name. That's cool, I guess. Dad's on an overseas business trip for the next four to six weeks. Right! Dad's in some undisclosed location. I miss Dad. I sure hope he's safe.

Okay, back to details. My grandparents died before I was born. Died? How can I say that? This is way too hard! Ugh, why did this have to happen? How can I do this? I'm only ten. What do they expect?

Mom says that people are resilient when a facing a challenge. This is bigger than any challenge I've ever encountered. I don't panic when I'm performing. Like that will be happening anytime soon! Focus, Richard. Why did they have to pick Richard? Richard James Baker. Richie, for short? Don't like the sound of that either. I guess I'll just stick with Richard.

What about Uncle Seth? Do I pretend he doesn't even exist? He's probably going out of his mind by now. He was supposed to come over for dinner. We were going to meet his girlfriend. Mom said they were pretty serious. Maybe I will finally have an aunt. Stay focused! I live at 246 River Cross Drive, Apartment 5C, Portland, Oregon. We moved here from Waco, Texas. Texas, really?

Are they going to believe me? Would I believe me? I can do this. Yes, I can do this. I'll never forget last Friday for as long as I live. On that Friday, I was Preston Alexander Davis. I was born July twelfth, not the twenty-first. I had blonde hair and blue eyes. Mom let me wear my hair a bit longer than Dad liked, but he eventually got used to it. Mila, my sister's real name, thought the long hair made me look more like an authentic musician.

And that's what I am at heart—or was—a musician. I've heard people say that I am a child prodigy since I was four. I'm not entirely sure what that means. Mom says it's when a child is automatically exceptional at something. All I know is that I really love music and playing the cello. Music comes from deep within me. When I play, I feel like nothing else matters. It's what I love more than anything. Playing the cello is what I am meant to do. It's my life.

At least, it was. I'm not sure about anything anymore. I was, and still am, a pretty solid student. Math, reading, science, social studies … I enjoy them all. Art is pretty cool too. Mrs. Nelson, my former art teacher, entered a few of my pieces in the last three county fairs. I even earned a first place ribbon last year. Sports? Well, let's just say I enjoy watching more than participating. My mom says that I have a proclivity—that's her word—for the arts and that's what makes me, me. Honestly, I wish I could be better at sports. My friends at The Briarcliffe School for the Performing Arts didn't care about my sports ability or lack of it. They were super supportive of my music. I guess a few of them were prodigies too. Giancarlo is the most incredible guitarist. For fun, he could transform a classical piece into a rock anthem without losing a beat. And Valerie, wow! She is a bona fide concert violinist. She's already played at Carnegie Hall—twice!

This was going to be my year—the year I was going to play at Carnegie Hall. But now they'll probably ask Brian Panabakker. He's pretty good. Okay, he's better than pretty good, but he's never been first chair. I have held that position since the age of four! I've got to stay focused. Stay focused, Preston! I mean Richard. Yikes, this is going to be impossible.

CHAPTER SEVEN

THREE DAYS EARLIER — FRIDAY, APRIL 13TH

I WILL NEVER FORGET the events of Friday, April 13th. Yes, you heard right—Friday the thirteenth! I was home early from rehearsal that afternoon, and Mila had canceled her sleepover plans with her "BFF" Layla because Uncle Seth was coming for dinner. We were finally going to meet his girlfriend, Megan. Mom told us that he had something important to tell us.

"Hey, Preston. Do you think Uncle Seth is engaged?" Mila asked me.

"That's probably the big news!" I exclaimed. Uncle Seth is one of my favorite people in the world. He's so much fun. Uncle Seth has this way of playing sports with me that makes me laugh. I think he's just as bad at sports as I am!

"It would be so cool to have an aunt. Aunt Megan and Uncle Seth. I like it! She'll probably be just as cool as Uncle Seth," Mila added.

"Your Uncle Seth is too much of a character to marry a bump on a log," Mom said. "Okay, you two, time to set the table," she added.

"Which dishes?" Mila asked.

"Use the ones in the dining room hutch."

"Oooh, she's going all fancy on us," I interjected with a laugh.

"Hey, it's not every day that your Uncle Seth brings a lady over and says he has a big announcement," Mom said.

"Mom has a point, Preston. And she's making her famous glazed pork roast with garlic potatoes. Your favorite," Mila said with a mischievous glance at me.

"We do have my news to celebrate," I said as I grabbed a handful of forks and knives from the drawer.

"You mean that invite to that small auditorium in New York?" Mom asked with a smirk.

"Barely worth me missing my soccer game," Mila added, wearing the same smirk. "Small auditorium? It's Carnegie Hall, Mom! That's pretty big," I said, looking at them in disbelief. They both began laughing. I couldn't help it. I started laughing too. Then the doorbell rang, followed by loud knocking. That wasn't Uncle Seth's style. He liked coming to the backyard and popping his head in the window over the sink. This would startle Mom or whoever was there. One time, he got Dad real good. I never heard Dad scream like that before. We still taunt him about it. The knocking continued. I guess Uncle Seth was putting his best foot forward now that he was bringing a lady for us to meet. He sure was relentless.

"I'm coming! I'm coming," I called out, racing to the door and pulling it open. But it wasn't Uncle Seth. Not even close.

"You must be Preston. Please have your mom come to the door," said the taller of the two men standing on our front stoop.

"Do I know you?" I asked, scanning my memory for any clues about who this man might be.

"No. It's urgent that we speak with Nicole

Montgomery Davis, wife of Timothy Lance Davis. We know she is here along with your sister Mila Davis. I must insist that we step inside as we need to proceed quickly," the man said quite calmly. His smile didn't sync with his words.

"Mom!" I called out as the two men stepped inside. My voice cracked slightly, making my face burn with embarrassment.

"Let Uncle Seth in, Preston. I'll be right out," she called back from the kitchen.

"Mom ... it's not Uncle Seth," I said, starting to feel a bit sick to my stomach.

"Who is it then?" she asked.

"Ma'am," the man called out. His voice seemed to echo through the room. Mom was out of the kitchen in a flash at the sound of his voice.

"My husband is upstairs on the phone—" Mom started to say before she was interrupted.

"Ma'am, your husband is with my department. We are from the United States Marshals Service, and we need a quick word with you in private,"

"I need to see identification right now," Mom said.

"Yes, ma'am," he said, pulling out an

official looking ID. Mom's face grew pale. The shorter man put out his hand and said, "Mrs. Davis, I'm Marshal Stevens. Here's my ID. Your husband is fine. We just need a word with you, and we don't have much time."

"Preston, wait with Mila in the family room." Mom appeared calm, but she was good at remaining calm during a crisis, so you could never really know what she was feeling on the inside. In her type of work, a crisis is an every-day occurrence. Sometimes it would truly be a crisis, but more often than not, it was a client worrying about whether or not they picked the right tile or light fixture. Mom was calm in those times, and today seemed no different.

"What did those men say to you, Preston?" Mila asked me as she began pacing nervously.

"They just said that they needed to speak with Mom. They knew all of our names. When Mom tried to pretend that Dad was upstairs, one guy told her that Dad was with his depart-ment ... the United States Marshals something ... I can't remember exactly what he said, but it freaked me out!"

"This has something to do with Dad's job, I just know it!"

"What do you mean?"

"Remember that day when Dad wasn't acting like himself?"

"Yeah, what about it?"

"I overheard him talking with Mom. He mentioned something about the new investors wanting to get an experimental drug the lab was testing approved by the FDA and on the market before the fourth quarter. He told Mom that it wasn't ready for human consumption and that he was being pressured to complete the study."

"Dad is the best bio-chemist. I'm sure they listened to him."

"I don't think so. He was ready to quit last Friday."

"He was? How do you know?"

"He mentioned something to me when we were driving home from soccer practice Saturday morning."

"Dad doesn't normally cave when the pressure is on."

"I know. But I think something bad was happening. He wouldn't say what it was when I asked him. He just told me that in this case what I don't know can't come back to harm me. It didn't make any sense. I'm really worried about Dad! This is freaking me out!"

"I hear them coming."

"We need to leave now," Mom said as she entered the room with the two men.

"The vehicle is parked out back. We must move quickly, no time to waste," said Marshal Stevens.

"What about Uncle Seth?" I asked.

"Don't worry about Uncle Seth," Mom responded.

"Where are you going?" Marshal Stevens asked Mila as she started up the stairs.

"I'm going to grab my phone," Mila responded, turning to Mom for support.

"No phones. We leave now," said Marshal Stevens.

"Mom, Layla is going to call me later."

"Honey, we need to listen to Marshal Stevens. I'll explain later, I promise." As we were walking out the door, I noticed that Mom didn't take her purse. Why were we being taken away so suddenly from our home? Where was Dad? How was Uncle Seth supposed to find us? I felt like we were being kidnapped. This was a total nightmare, and I wanted it to be over!

CHAPTER EIGHT

RAK INITIATIVE

"R.J., HOW ARE YOU feeling now?" Nurse Mitchell asked while placing her hand on my shoulder. "It looks like you've been deep in thought. Are you sure nothing else is bothering you?"

"Yes, ma'am, I'm sure. I think you were right about being dehydrated. I feel much better now," I answered with a glance at the clock above the door. I had been lying there longer than I realized and dismissal was quickly approaching. "I'd better get back to class before the bell rings," I said as I sat up slowly and then stood up cautiously.

"Well, I guess that might be a good idea, but my door is open to you if you ever need a listening ear."

Nurse Mitchell was the kind of person who made you feel comfortable without a fuss. I must admit that resting in her office was the most comfortable I've felt since this whole witness protection protocol started. Protocol, that was the word Marshal Stevens used when he debriefed us Friday night on our way to the private airport. It was a word that I've heard in the superhero movies that Dad and I have watched this year. Maybe Dad and the rest of us have been part of a superhero movie this whole time. Now that would be cool. If only that were true.

Mr. Bailey was already lining up the students when I made it back to the classroom. I was hoping to avoid any conversation about the earlier events. My goal was to put up my chair, grab my backpack, line up, and get on the bus without having to speak with anyone. Andy, Sophie, and Jennilee had already cleaned off my work area, put up my chair, and gathered my belongings before I made it back to class. Andy handed my backpack to me as I passed by him, so I joined the back of the line.

"Great to have you back, Mr. Baker!

Your first day has proven to be quite memorable. Remember to keep hydrated because we need you, my friend!" Mr. Bailey pointed at me and smiled, then looked down at his clipboard. "Class, I have some reminders before you go. Tomorrow is Day 2. We have music and normal recess. The other three classes will practice tomorrow, but we're back on the field on Wednesday! Also, remember to complete the math word problems on your Google Drive. For those of you still needing to complete your RAK post, we only have six more weeks. R.J., you'll find directions on how to access the drive at home along with some information about the RAK project in your homework folder. Jennilee made sure your homework folder is in your backpack, so you should be set. That's it, folks! Have a great evening." Just as he finished, the second bell rang, and we were off down the hall to the bus loop.

"Which bus do you ride?" Andy asked as we approached the loop.

"Bus 108," I answered.

"Too bad! Jennilee, Sophie, and I ride bus 85. I guess we'll see you tomorrow," Andy said, giving a quick wave of his hand.

"Yeah, tomorrow," I paused, "see you

then." I tried to seem enthusiastic, but I don't think I was too successful. This new life was so different. I want my old life back, and I really need to see Dad.

Boarding the bus, I quickly made my way toward the back, avoiding eye contact with anyone. I heard two boys laughing as I walked past. They continued to laugh and occasionally look back at me for most of the ride. I knew they were talking about me. I could feel it even though I couldn't hear what they were saying. They got off a few stops before me, so I had some reprieve. Would I need to experience this again tomorrow? Maybe Mom's new job will let her come and get me so I won't have to ride the bus. I could be a car rider. That would definitely help make this whole experience more tolerable. I will bring this up at dinner tonight. Mom will fix it, just like she's does for her clients. At least, I hope so.

CHAPTER NINE

LAUGHTER ISN'T ALWAYS THE BEST MEDICINE

"YOU'RE WORRIED ABOUT TWO boys laughing at you on the bus. Are you kidding me? Do you realize how hard it is to go to a new high school, let alone in April? Everyone's in their own clique. I'm the outsider! I don't fit in! You have no idea how much I miss Layla and the rest of my friends! If this is hard for you, then it's ten times worse for me! Get a grip, Preston—I mean R.J.!"

"Honey, I know this is hard for you, but it's just as hard for R.J. You need to stop and think about his sacrifices—finishing the last quarter of fifth grade without his friends, not to mention Carnegie—"

"I know, Mom! You're right. Sorry, R.J. I'm not mad at you. It's just that this whole thing is so much harder than I had expected. I'm worried about Dad. Uncle Seth is probably worried sick." Mallory stopped talking and looked at me with concern. "Why were those boys laughing at you? Did something happen? Are they in your class?"

"No, they're not in my class. The students in my class seem really friendly, especially my teammates, Andy, Sophie, and Jennilee."

"So, why were those boys laughing at you?"

"Something happened at recess today. There's this kickball competition coming up between all the fifth grade—"

"Oh, now I get it! Sorry, R.J., I could only imagine what happened. I know how bad you are at sports."

"Mallory!" Mom interjected.

"No, Mom, Mallory is right. I've got two left feet when it comes to sports, and you know it too. You're the one who said that I have a proclivity for the arts instead of sports."

"I like how you remembered the exact

word I used—proclivity. And I was right. We are all different and so are our talents. I'm so proud of both of you, and I truly hate that you have to make this sacrifice. We must focus on Dad and all that he has to face over the next four weeks. If all goes well, there's a chance we can go back to our old lives. Time will tell."

"But what if that doesn't happen?" Mallory asked with a worried look.

"Honey, let's take it one day at a time. No need to worry about it now. Dinner is getting cold, and I made your favorites. Let's eat before I have to warm it all up again."

I couldn't hold in my feelings any longer. I felt like we were all stuck inside a bad dream. I wanted so badly to wake up and realize that it really was just a dream, a really awful one. "Has Dad called? I'm just wondering why we're not talking about him. He should have called by now. We haven't seen him since last Friday morning. Am I the only one who's freaking out about not seeing Dad? I'm just worried that I'll never see him again."

"Oh, honey, of course we're all worried about Dad. It's just safer not to discuss the details so one of us doesn't slip up and give us away. According to Marshal Stevens, Dad is safe and doing well."

"How do we know that he's telling us the truth?" asked Mallory, fighting back tears.

"We don't even know these men. What if they work for those shady investors and this is part of their master plan? We can't even contact Uncle Seth or Grandma and Grandpa. This is worse than prison." At this point, tears were streaming down my face. With all that had happened since Friday, I just couldn't hold them back any longer.

"Come here, you two." Mom put her arms around both of us, and we all began to sob. "You two are the most important people in our lives. Dad and I love you beyond words, and we would sacrifice our own lives for yours. I know your Dad. He is resilient, confident, and more determined than any person I've ever known. We will see him soon, and he will be fine. All of us will be just fine. Right now we need to focus on being strong for Dad and each other. It's not going to be easy—have you noticed the way this place is decorated? I could have done better blindfolded and both hands tied behind my back!"

Our sobs instantly turned to laughter. Mom knew how to cheer us up. She was right about it not being easy. I missed my music just as much as I missed Dad, and the thought of having to play kickball again was almost too much to bear. But for Dad's safety, I was willing to try.

"I love you, Mom, and you too, R.J.," Mallory said as she wiped her face with a tissue and made her way to her seat at the table. "Let's have dinner. We can't let our favorites go to waste!"

"Yeah, I concur! And I love you, Mom, and Mal—can I call you Mal for short?" I asked.

"Why not, just as long as it doesn't morph into malady, malice, or something else you might think is clever."

"I thought you supported my cleverness."

"No, I support your musical talents, not your rudeness!"

"Okay, okay! No malaria then?" I asked with a straight face.

"Don't push it, Richard!"

"Okay, you two. Dinner is officially cold. Give me a minute to warm things up in the microwave." Mom covered the serving plate with a wet paper towel and put it in the microwave.

"So, Mom … do you think you can pick me up tomorrow?" I asked, hoping to hear an answer that would make school more tolerable.

"It appears that I will be working the morning shift at the flower shop, at least until mid-May. Misty Chapman, the owner, will be touring Northern Europe with her sister for the next three weeks. She was impressed by my skills and asked if I could cover her shift until she returned." Before becoming a successful interior designer, Mom made it through college working in a flower shop.

"That will be great, Mom!" Mallory announced, dumping a heaping spoonful of mashed potatoes on her plate. "The girls' soccer team has an opening. I was thinking of trying out tomorrow afternoon. If I make it, I'll need you to pick me up from practices around five-ish."

"The soccer team? Don't you think that will give you away?" I asked, glancing at Mom.

"I'm not a child prodigy like you, R.J. Trust me, no one will guess my true identity by playing on the girls' soccer team."

"She's right, R.J. Don't get me wrong, Mallory is an amazing soccer player, but her photos and story haven't been featured in newspapers and magazines for the last six years."

"On second thought, I think I'll forget about trying out," Mallory said.

"Why? Mom just said that it wouldn't give away your identity."

"I just realized that it wouldn't be fair to you. I don't want to be selfish."

"Just do it, Mallory. At least something about our lives will be familiar." I was grateful for her gesture. I know she is really missing her friends, especially Layla. Truth be told, I heard her crying last night when I walked past her room going down the hall to the bathroom. After seeing her break down about Dad, I knew this was pretty hard for her too. On Sunday, Mom didn't let her create a fake Facebook account so she could check on her friends. Mom told us that the U.S. Marshal recommended that all social media be avoided until further notice. I couldn't care less, but Instagram and Facebook were Mallory's sidekicks. Sometimes I need to be reminded that it's not just about me.

After dinner, I used Mr. Bailey's directions to access the math word problems. They were fairly simple for me. I also checked out the RAK uploads on his website. I saw Andy, Sophie, and Jennilee's posts and read a few others before logging off. The posts were all pretty good, especially Andy's. He befriended a boy with Down's Syndrome earlier in the school year and now spends a couple afternoons a week playing video games with him and just shooting the breeze. I think the best part of his post was when he wrote, "Ben has made me a better person. When I look at him now, I see a great friend, not a kid with a disability." It's only been one day, but I could tell that Andy was a decent kid and potentially a good friend.

I could feel my eyes grow heavy as soon as my head hit the pillow. Before I could complete my prayers, I drifted off to sleep. It seemed like no time passed before it was morning again and time to face a new day. At least our class didn't have the field at recess, so no kickball practice today.

CHAPTER TEN

MUSIC WITH MRS. WELLS

THE FIRST FEW HOURS of school on Tuesday were uneventful, much like the first part of Monday. I actually got through a few more chapters in *Mr. Popper's Penguins* before the center rotations were over. On the even days, our class had specials right after the reading block. On odd days, it was at the very end of the day, so I missed art on Monday afternoon when I was in the nurse's office. Mr. Bailey had us take a quick bathroom break before we made our way to the music room. Mrs. Wells, the music teacher, greeted us at the entrance of the music room. She looked really young, but

Sophie told me she had two kids in high school, so I guess she just looked young.

The music room was better than expected. It was rather large, compared to the regular classrooms anyway. There were keyboards placed along the back wall and a large assortment of percussion instruments along the wall with windows. At the front of the room there was a display of stringed instruments—ukulele, acoustic guitar, bass guitar, banjo, violin, viola, cello, and bass. It was an impressive display. Not what I would have imagined for a public elementary school. Seeing the cello just feet away from me was total torture. Of all weeks to begin at Fern Creek Elementary, here I was the week the music classes were going to learn about stringed instruments. We sat in assigned seats, and Mrs. Wells began class by introducing the name of each instrument. She actually played each one quite masterfully.

"Now that you've heard the name of each instrument and how they sound when played, I'm going to let you listen to a series of classical pieces. After listening for a few minutes, I will ask you to tell me which instrument is being featured. Does anyone have any questions before we begin?"

Thomas's hand shot up, and before Mrs. Wells could call on him, he blurted, "Do we get a prize if we name them all correctly?"

"Mr. Fisher, must I still remind you to wait until I call on you before asking a question?"

"Sorry, Mrs. Wells. It's just that I remembered my older brother telling me that his class won a prize when they correctly matched all the instruments to the songs you played when he was in fifth grade!"

"That's right, your brother's class has been the only one to do that on first try, so I did get them a prize. I believe I had my husband's cousin come by with his ice cream truck."

"Yes, you did. He said that they got to pick whatever they wanted! Can we do the same?"

"Let's take it one step at a time, Mr. Fisher. If you all succeed, then we can talk." Mrs. Wells gave the class a smile and with a little flourish of her fingers pressed play on her computer.

The first five pieces were quite easy to distinguish even for an amateur musician. Mrs. Wells chose five different students, and each time they answered correctly. The next selection had most of the students looking confused. I recognized the piece immediately as I had played it during a recital when I was five. It was Bach's Cello Suite No. 1 The Prelude. I had earned a Superior rating on my performance and a standing ovation. I guess you could say that it was a defining moment in my life. Standing there as a little kid, I knew that music was my true love, and the cello was my voice.

Once I heard someone say that most people don't experience their defining moment until they are much older, and some don't ever experience it at all. I couldn't imagine being one of those people who never have that opportunity. It's probably the best thing anyone could ever experience.

But now I was not sure what was worse— not to have that moment or to have had it and have to pretend that it never happened. I knew the musical answer when no one else did, but I couldn't say anything for fear of revealing my true identity. Scanning the room, I noticed one girl staring intently at me. As the seconds continue to pass with no one raising a hand, I could see her growing more agitated. After what seemed like an eternity, Mrs. Wells said, "It doesn't seem like any of you know the instrument featured in this piece. It's the—"

"Cello!" the girl interjected before Mrs. Wells finished.

"Yes, that is correct, Ella! You sure waited until the last minute to answer, but that makes six out of six correct," Mrs. Wells said. Ella gave me one last glance, shook her head, and went on listening. The seventh and ninth pieces featured instruments already named—the violin and the banjo. The eighth piece featured the viola and the tenth was the ukulele, both of which were recognized correctly.

"Mr. Bailey's class, I am quite impressed," Mrs. Wells said when the final correct answer was given. "You are the second class ever to get them all correct on the first try. I think I will be speaking with my husband's cousin this evening."

With those words the class began to cheer. They had done it without my help. I must admit it was impressive for a regular school. This would have been a no brainer for the students at The Briarcliffe School for the Performing Arts because they lived and breathed the arts day in and day out. Most of them could name each piece and composer within five seconds. But I really didn't expect much here at Fern Creek Elementary. Maybe I was wrong.

Mr. Bailey, hearing the cheering, walked into the room and asked, "So, what's all the cheering about, Mrs. Wells?"

"Mr. Bailey, I'm glad you stepped in. Your class is the second group in all the years that I've been teaching at Fern Creek to recognize all the stringed instruments featured in various music selections correctly on the first attempt. I'm so impressed!"

"They are a special group, Mrs. Wells. They soar in all academic areas and soon will be the reigning kickball champs of fifth grade!" Mr. Bailey spoke with a certainty that made me feel uneasy. I was going to be the one to ruin his chances of keeping the trophy on the shelf behind his desk. That was not a defining moment I wanted to experience.

That afternoon it stormed, so we had indoor recess. I played chess with Andy while Sophie and Jennilee drew in their journals. Occasionally, I spotted Ella looking my way. I couldn't understand why she was staring at me. It was like she was mad, disappointed, or something along those lines. I haven't done anything to her—at least I don't think I have. Maybe I was reading too much into it. After all, I had only been at this school for two days. With all that was happening in my life at the moment, I didn't need any more drama.

CHAPTER ELEVEN

YOU NEED A SHOWER

THE EVENING WAS MUCH quieter than it was the night before. Mom picked me up in the car rider line, so I was able to avoid the pointing and snickering on the bus. Mallory stayed at school for tryouts, so the apartment was quiet for a few hours. I decided to take a short nap before finishing my homework. Mom had picked up a simple MP3 player and added some of my favorite classical pieces. I put on the earbuds, made myself cozy on the couch, pressed play, and closed my eyes. A tranquil feeling filled my body as I imagined myself siting off center stage at Carnegie Hall.

The neck of a new Eastman cello rested in my left hand, the bow in my right. Here, I didn't lack confidence and I wasn't afraid. I could live here, and for the next thirty or so minutes, I did.

Mallory pulled out my earbuds and my imagined reality came to an abrupt halt. "It looks like you had a wrestling match with some mud, Mal."

"Yeah, the field was pretty wet, so I slipped a few times during tryouts."

"Well, how did it go?" I asked, already knowing the answer.

"It was so awesome! The Varsity coach thanked me at least five times for trying out. He said that I was definitely on the team."

"Of course! I didn't expect anything different." On the soccer field, Mallory was a star. Soccer was her thing. Playing gave her the same centered feeling I experienced on the stage. We were different, yet we were similar. I wouldn't be surprised if she earned a full soccer scholarship to college.

"Mom said dinner will be ready in about forty-five minutes. Did you finish your homework?" asked Mallory.

"No, not yet. I don't have too much to

get done. Forty-five minutes should be plenty of time," I answered.

"I'm going to take a shower. After dinner, I'll finish the last few math problems I didn't get done before tryouts."

"Glad to hear it! You look and smell pretty bad. It's a malady that can be avoided by some good old fashioned soap and water." I knew she would get riled at that, but I couldn't help it.

"Ha ha! You think you're so funny." Her sarcasm was alive and well.

"It was a simple slip of the tongue, nothing intentional."

"Yeah, right! Whatever you say, Richard," she said as she pretended to hug me.

"Hey, don't touch me with your smelly, muddy body!" I protested.

"This time you're off the hook. Next time, well ... I can't make any promises."

"Okay, Okay! You win. No more name morphing, Mal." She did smell pretty bad.

After completing my homework, I helped Mom set the table. She seemed to be lost in her thoughts. She's strong, but everyone is entitled to a weak moment. I knew she was worried about Dad. They've known each other since their freshman year in high school and have barely spent any time apart since they married a little over eighteen years ago. Their friends call them the "Power Couple." They are both very successful and, in my opinion, the best parents in the universe. The silence was interrupted by Mal's call from her bedroom.

"Mom! Is it okay if I use your hairdryer?"

"Sure, honey. But hurry up, dinner is ready," Mom replied.

"I just need a few minutes."

Mom and I made our way to the table. The spaghetti and meatballs smelled delicious. I hadn't felt hungry until I sat down at the dinner table. Just as I was about to call out to my sister to hurry up, she popped into the room, making a grand entrance. She was wearing a Forest Ridge soccer team shirt.

"What do you think?"

"Oh, honey, it looks great!"

"You might want to wear something different since we're having spaghetti tonight." I thought I should warn her. She seemed too excited about being on the team to think about sauce stains.

"Good idea, little brother. I forgive you."

"I'm curious. What do you forgive him for?" Mom asked.

"His *mal*intent earlier," Mallory said as she raced back to her room to change her shirt.

"Oh, I see. Glad to hear you're working it out," Mom called after her.

As Mallory dropped into her chair, Mom said, "Who wants to say grace?"

"I'll do it," Mallory volunteered.

"Thanks, Mallory," Mom said.

We grabbed hands and bowed our heads.

"Dear God. Thank you for watching over us and for keeping Dad safe. Also thank you for helping me make the team today. I ask that you help Mom enjoy her job at the Flower Shop and that R.J. has a moment to shine. And most of all, we ask that you bring Dad home to us. Bless this food and let it be nourishing to our bodies. Oh, and please don't let the family and friends we can't contact freak out too badly. Amen."

"Amen," Mom and I said in unison.

Mom may look different and be working a different job, but her talent in the kitchen was intact. There was not one speck of food left on any of our plates, and we even had seconds! The only thing that would have made this dinner better would have been Dad and his lame jokes at the table with us. What I wouldn't give for one of those lame jokes right about now.

CHAPTER TWELVE

THE NOTE

I WAS HAVING THE coolest dream when
Mom's voice woke me up. We had overslept!
The clock on my nightstand was blinking, the
telltale sign of a power outage sometime during
the night.

"We only have twenty minutes to be
ready and out the door!" Mom called out. Mallory had her shower last night, so I ran into the
bathroom and took a lightning-fast shower. I
didn't want to be late, especially since I was still
the new kid. By the time I got out, Mom had
protein shakes made for each of us. She was
brilliant that way. Mallory and I grabbed our

backpacks and shakes and headed for the car. Just as Mom was about to grab her car keys and protein shake, the special cell phone given to us by Marshal Stevens rang. Mom hesitated for just a moment before answering.

"Hello, this is Candice Baker." There was a brief pause. "Yes. I understand. Thank you for the update. Please let him know ... yes, that's fine. Good-bye." When Mom opened the car door, we knew she had heard some news about Dad.

"Can you tell us anything?" Mallory asked, hoping for some good news.

"Well, all I can say is that today is a pretty big day for him. So far, all has gone as planned. Say a prayer every time you think of him today. Okay?"

"Of course, Mom," Mallory answered, grabbing my hand. "R.J. and I will be on it."

I think I said about a half dozen prayers for Dad before we reached Fern Creek Elementary. I just wanted to be sure that God heard me. Mom pulled up to the curb just as the first bell was ringing.

"You better hurry, champ!"

"I will, Mom. See you later."

I made it to class just as the second bell

rang. I opened my backpack, pulled out my homework folder, and hung the backpack on the hook in my cubby. As I took down my chair, a folded note fell to the ground.

"Hey, you dropped something!" Jennilee whispered as I looked down to see what it was.

"Thanks. I got it," I said, wondering what it could be. Mr. Bailey was taking attendance, so I took the opportunity to open the folded note. There were only five words written neatly on the paper.

I know your secret. Ella

I instantly felt sick. How did she know my secret? What did I do to give it away? I was so careful. Will I ever be able to see Dad again?

The morning dragged on and on, and I could barely recall hearing a single thing. My mind was completely consumed by the words on that note and what could happen to Dad if the "investors" knew our new identities. I continued to pray over and over in my head, hoping that God could fix what I had messed up.

"Mr. Baker. Mr. Baker!" Mr. Bailey was trying to get my attention, but I was buried too deep in thought to hear him. A sharp kick on my shin from Andy finally broke me from my trance.

"Yes, Mr. Bailey."

"May I speak with you for a moment, R.J.?"

"Yes, sir." I walked over to Mr. Bailey, and he led me into the hall.

"Is everything okay with you? You seem completely lost in your thoughts this morning."

"Oh, sorry, Mr. Bailey. It's just that, well ... I ..."

"It's okay if you don't want to share. I just want to make sure you know I am here for you if you need me."

"I know that, sir. I guess it's been hard getting used to all the changes, and my dad is away on a business trip ... so I miss him. And this morning, the alarm didn't go off."

"Hey, I get it. You've been through a ton of changes in a short time. Use today's kickball practice as a way of letting off some of the stress of the week."

Mr. Bailey was trying to be helpful, and it had been working until he mentioned kickball practice.

"Maybe I should just sit out today," I suggested.

"Nonsense. There's nothing like a good kickball game to take away all your worries.

I know he meant well, but at that moment I just wanted to disappear into my music.

"Okay, Mr. Bailey. I'm sure you're right. Thanks for caring."

"R.J., are you sure there's nothing else?"

"Yes, sir."

"Well, if you think of anything at any point, I'm always available."

"Thank you, Mr. Bailey." His genuineness was evident. I just wished he could see that even the thought of playing kickball was too much for me. Maybe if it was just for fun, but for competition—I couldn't convince myself I could do it.

Before long, it was lunch time. When I was paying the cashier for my food, I noticed Ella waiting for me.

"Hey, come sit over here. I asked Mr. Bailey for permission, and he thought it would be a great idea." Ella was determined to make this day a complete disaster.

"Okay," I responded and followed her. We sat across from each other, and for the first five minutes, not a single word was exchanged between us. Ella finally broke the silence with a question.

"Did you get my note?"

"Yes," I replied.

"Did you read it?" she asked.

"Yes."

"So, did you figure out how I know?"

"No, not really."

"I guess you didn't recognize my little sister on Monday," she added.

"Huh?" I asked, not getting her clue.

"You know, the little kindergartener who gave you a hug in the hallway when Mrs. Grant was walking you to the classroom."

"That was your sister?"

"Yes! She recognized you first."

"She did?" At this point I was completely confused.

"I didn't see it until music on Tuesday. When you didn't raise your hand, I was confused, but then I figured you were not a show-off. Of course, I would have thrown something at you if we hadn't won because you didn't answer," she said quite matter-of-factly.

"Are you kidding?"

"No. Of all people, you probably not only knew the instrument featured but the name of each piece by hearing the first few notes."

"What makes you say that?"

"Okay, I'm going to try to get through

this without crying. Don't judge me if I can't."

"I won't judge," I said.

"My older sister, Mickey, was a talented violinist and often performed in local competitions."

"She *was* a talented violinist?" I asked, emphasizing the word was.

"Yes, she died last year from a rare heart condition."

"Oh, I'm so sorry ..."

"Thank you. Let me finish while I can. We moved here last summer, right before school started. My mom and dad thought it would be good for us to have a new start. Before that, we lived in Seattle. Last October, we were invited to the Seattle Symphony for a performance in honor of my sister, and you played the cello solo."

"But that was for a girl named Michelle, not Mickey," I said without thinking.

"Mickey is what we called her. Her name was Michelle," Ella explained.

"Oh, now I get why your sister's hug gave me déjà vu. She hugged me that night. She came out of the crowd and just held onto me."

"She recognized you the moment she saw you. I can't say that I did. You look sort of different. I think your hair is shorter and darker. When I heard your name on Monday morning, I didn't make any connections. Then on Monday evening, after Natalia told us that she hugged the cello player from Mickey's special concert, we all began looking for the program from that evening.

"We had no luck. Mom thinks it might have been in the bag that the airline permanently lost on our trip home. Your name didn't ring a bell with Mom either when I mentioned it to her. But then again, how many people can remember names, especially in this case when we were all emotional about my sister. It really clicked during music class. That's when I knew it was you—the cello guy."

As I listened to Ella explain how she knew my secret, I was glad to know she didn't remember my real name. What a relief. Maybe I hadn't compromised our safety after all.

"Your sister has a really good memory. I just can't believe that you didn't remember a simple name like R.J. But under the circumstances, I completely understand."

"So, where are you playing now?"

"Well, I'm not playing at the moment. I decided to take a break for a while, maybe try something new. Can I ask you a favor?"

"Sure," she responded.

"Can you keep this our secret?"

"I get it. I was the new kid earlier this year. Sure, no problem."

"Thanks!" I said, breathing a sigh of relief.

"So, are you into sports? You didn't seem too excited about kickball on Monday. I mean you fainted, but I don't think that was from excitement. Am I right?"

"Yeah ..." I hesitated. "I'm not too confident with sports. This game seems really important to Mr. Bailey, and I'd hate to be the one to make us lose."

"Nah, how bad can you be? Let's see how practice goes today," she said.

CHAPTER THIRTEEN

A THORN IN MY SIDE

KICKBALL PRACTICE WAS ALMOST a repeat of Monday's tragic event with the exception of one detail—I didn't faint. Instead, while running toward the oncoming ball, my legs fumbled over it, causing me to land face first in the dirt. The stinging pain was no match for the sting that rose from sheer embarrassment. Once again, I could hear the laughter from a group of Mrs. Granger's students, followed by some unflattering comments. I had never experienced bullying before, although I knew that it happened. My parents spared me from this kind of thing by sending me to The Briarcliffe

School for the Performing Arts, starting in pre-school. I fit in there. Everyone was a friend.

I remember the stories Trey and Emily, two of my closest friends since second grade, shared about their school experience prior to attending Briarcliffe. They hated school before then. I couldn't comprehend why anyone would make fun of Trey. He was what they call a triple threat—someone who excels in at least three different areas. In Trey's case, he excelled in sports, acting, and dancing. In fact, I think his dance background helped him on the football field. At least, that's what my dad always said.

"I guess you plan on being a regular customer, Mr. Baker," Nurse Mitchell said as she cleaned a few abrasions on my right cheek. "Kickball doesn't seem to be a good fit for you."

She was definitely right about that. Kickball was quickly become a thorn in my side.

"Yeah, I guess my timing is off."

"There are quite a few excellent kickball players in your class. I'm sure they can give you some tips if you ask," Nurse Mitchell offered as she handed me an ice pack. "Keep that ice pack on your right cheek until dismissal. That should help with any swelling."

"Yes, ma'am. May I head back to class now?"

"Of course, Mr. Baker. In the future, try to stay away from the ground with your head," she said smiling.

"I'll try. Thank you!"

"You're very welcome. See you next time," she said, giving me a wink.

Heading back to class, I kept wondering how much ridicule I would receive from my classmates. Would they finally realize that I shouldn't play kickball if they wanted to win? I bet some of them secretly hoped I would be transferred to another homeroom. To my surprise, everyone appeared preoccupied with the science inquiry Mr. Bailey had presented in my absence. No one said a word to me. A few students waved to me as I walked past, and Ella handed me a note when I walked by her table. I tucked the note in my pocket before Mr. Bailey noticed and headed straight for my table. My teammates were working together on the inquiry and seemed happy to see me.

"I hope you're good in science, R.J.," Andy said as I scooted my seat in a bit closer.

"I think I'm fairly decent in science," I said.

I wanted to smile but my swollen cheek made that hard to do. "What is the inquiry question?"

Jennilee read aloud, "Which liquids do you believe will cause a chemical reaction with a penny and why?"

"Piece of cake! We did this at my old school."

"I knew you could help!" Sophie added, smiling at me.

"Which liquids are we using?" I asked, looking at the group.

"Distilled water, white vinegar, salt water, rubbing alcohol, and Pepsi," answered Andy.

"How do you know it's Pepsi and not Coke or something else?" Sophie asked sarcastically.

"I like to think of myself as a Pepsi aficionado," Andy retorted.

"A Pepsi what?" asked Sophie.

"A Pepsi aficionado—a person, in this case me, who knows a lot about Pepsi and it's amazing qualities."

"You're a dork!" announced Sophie.

"That's right, I'm a Pepsi aficionado dork!"

"Let's get back to the experiment before we get in trouble," Jennilee interjected, looking at me for support.

"She's right. We're already behind because of me."

"But you already know the answer," Andy said.

"Yes, but we won't learn anything if I just give you the answer. It needs to be a group effort."

"Yeah, he's right. You know how Mr. Bailey always asks each member of the group to explain their findings. If we let him write the answer, we won't know what to say," Jennilee explained.

"Okay, okay! You win. Let's get going, but save me some of that Pepsi. All this experimenting is making me thirsty." Andy smiled then began organizing the items as the rest of us discussed the properties of each liquid and the possible reactions they would have with the copper in a penny.

We worked straight through to the first dismissal bell, and before long, I was sitting in the passenger seat of Mom's car and heading home for the day. It was then that I remembered the note in my pocket. I needed to read it before doing anything else.

CHAPTER FOURTEEN

SHE KNOWS

AS MOM PULLED INTO our assigned parking spot in the apartment complex, I couldn't stop thinking about the note in my pocket. Mom had a few grocery bags in the trunk, so after helping her carry them inside, I made a beeline for my bedroom.

"Where are you going?" Mom asked.

"I'm going to change my shirt. I spilled some vinegar on it this afternoon while doing a science experiment."

"So that's why I'm craving a large tossed salad," Mom said with a laugh.

"Funny, Mom. I'll be back in a sec." I

closed the door to my room, pulled off my shirt, and grabbed the note from my pocket. The note was folded several times, and with every unfolding, I became more anxious. Did someone else know something about my secret? Had Ella blabbed what she knew to the other students? Finally, I got the note unfolded. It was from Ella. As I read it, I felt sick again.

R.J., I know another secret about you—you are not good at sports. Don't worry, I've only told a few close friends who want to help. They won't tell anyone else. I promise. I have a plan. We'll talk about it soon.

Your new friend, Ella

At this point, I didn't know which was harder—being in the witness protection program and forgoing a life-changing performance or having the students in Mr. Bailey's class find out I can't play kickball or any sport! I lay back on my bed wishing this could all just stop. For the next few minutes, I imagined Mom bursting into my room with news that Dad was fine and we were going back to our normal lives.

Instead, I was brought back to reality when I heard Mom calling me from the kitchen.

"R.J., I left a snack for you on the table. I need to head out shortly to pick up Mallory from soccer practice. Are you coming out?"

I grabbed a clean T-shirt from my dresser and pulled it over my head as I headed to the kitchen. I pushed the note back into my pocket.

"I'm here, Mom."

"I thought you might have dozed off. I didn't want to leave the snack out if you had fallen asleep."

"I couldn't decide on a shirt to wear."

"Are you kidding? It's not like you're going anywhere this evening."

"I guess I was just being too picky. You know me, always the perfectionist."

"Yes, I do know you and that's why I know this has nothing to do with which T-shirt to wear. You're missing your music and with the Carnegie Hall date approaching ..."

"Yes, but I know we need to be strong for Dad. It's just that ..."

"Did something else happen at school?"

At this point, I could feel my eyes flooding with tears. "Mom, some of the kids know I can't play sports!"

"Honey, I'm sure they won't care."

"No, Mom! You don't understand, there's this big kickball competition, and Mr. Bailey's students have been the reigning champions for the last two years. They plan to win again, but with me on the team, they don't stand a chance!"

"I'm sure they'll let you watch. After all, you just started."

"That's just it, Mom. I've tried to get out of it, but they're not having it. They're an all for one and one for all kind of class. Mr. Bailey is such a great teacher. He inspires everyone to do their best. I never imagined that I would encounter this kind of teacher outside of Briarcliffe. I can't stand the thought of letting him down."

"My goodness, I'm impressed. It's been less than a week and you feel this strongly."

"Yes, but I've also experienced bullying for the first time."

"From the students in your class?"

"No, they're in Mrs. Granger's fifth grade class. They're the ones who were talking and laughing about me on the bus. Every time they see me, they call me a loser or pretend to faint."

"Oh, I see. So, being a car rider hasn't really helped."

"Yes, it has! I only have to hear it when I pass them in the hallway."

"I can e-mail Mr. Bailey about it."

"No, that's not going to help! I need to learn how to play kickball!"

"Mi- I mean Mallory can probably help with that."

"She may be good at sports, but she doesn't have any patience. We'll make each other crazy!"

"You're probably right. I can try to help you."

"Mom, you crack me up!"

"Hey, watch it! I was pretty good at volleyball when I was in high school."

"I think someone might help me at school."

"Who?"

"This girl named Ella. She gave me this note today." I took the note out of my pocket and handed it to her. Mom unfolded it and read Ella's message.

"So, what was the first secret that she knew about you?"

"Oh, you noticed that ..."

"Yes, go on, spill the beans."

I took a deep breath then told Mom about the conversation I had with Ella during lunch. Mom listened intently, nodding her head occasionally. When I was finished, she sat there quietly. I could tell she was thinking. This went on for a few minutes before the deafening silence was broken.

"Are you sure she doesn't know your real name? That could put us in great danger."

"No, Mom. She said that her mom couldn't find the program from the concert in honor of her sister. She thinks it was in a suitcase that the airline permanently lost."

"So that cute little girl who hugged you on that night is her little sister?"

"Yes."

"She recognized you even though you look so different. How is that possible?"

"I don't know. She just knew somehow."

"That's pretty intuitive for a young child. On second thought, it makes perfect sense. She saw your spirit—who you are beyond the length and color of your hair. You do have a way of leaving an impression."

"I kind of told Ella that I was taking a break from playing the cello."

"How did she respond to that?"

"Not sure. She promised not to tell anyone about my secret and then went on to talk about kickball."

"So, how do you think Ella is going to help you with kickball?"

"I have no idea. I guess I'll find out tomorrow, probably at lunch."

Mom's phone alarm sounded, startling us both.

"That's my cue to pick up Mallory. Want to come with me?"

"No, I think I should get started on homework."

"Okay, just remember to put the plate in the dishwasher when you finish your snack."

Mom grabbed her purse and car keys and headed out to the car. I finished my snack, put the plate in the dishwasher as directed, and began working on homework. As I finished the last word problem and pulled out *Mr. Popper's Penguins* for a little reading time, I heard a knock at the door followed by the ringing of the doorbell. The combination was eerily familiar. Was this another visit from the U.S. Marshals?

CHAPTER FIFTEEN

AN UNEXPECTED VISIT

I WALKED HESITANTLY TO the door and peered through the peephole. To my surprise it wasn't Marshal Stevens or one of his cronies; it was Ella, Thomas, and Blake. What were they doing here? How did they know where I lived? I opened the door slowly and stood there as the three looked at me.

"Hey, R.J.!" Ella said.

"Hey!"

"Thomas and Blake are here with me to help you out."

"Huh?" I asked.

"The note ..." she said hesitantly. "You

know ... kickball."

"Oh, I thought we were going to talk about it tomorrow."

"No time to waste, my friend!" Thomas added as he put out a fist bump. I obliged and did the same with Blake.

"We can use the field beside the back parking lot. Thomas brought his kickball." Ella appeared determined.

"How did you know where I live?" I asked.

"Blake lives in the next set of apartments. He saw you move in last Saturday afternoon," she explained.

"Oh, so where do you two live?"

"We live in Fern Crest Hills, a large subdivision just a few blocks from the school. Ella lives in the house directly behind mine," answered Thomas.

"Yep, we're neighbors!" Ella added.

"So how did you two get here?"

"My mom dropped us off at Blake's apartment," Ella said. "We plan to help you learn to play kickball."

"Oh, well I ..."

"Hey, don't worry. It's cool with us. Not everyone excels at sports. But with some practice, anything is possible." Thomas sounded convincing, but I was still on the fence about the whole thing. Music and academics came naturally to me, but it would take a miracle to feel confident about playing sports.

"Let's go! We only have about an hour before my mom picks us up," Ella said as she grabbed my arm.

"Hold on, I need to grab my key and leave a note for my mom. She went to pick up my sister." I ran into my bedroom and grabbed my apartment key. I quickly scribbled a note to Mom and hung it on the fridge door with a magnet. I locked the door behind me, and the four of us headed to the grassy area.

"I'm really, really bad at this." This was the hardest personal fact that I ever revealed to someone other than my immediate family, but it was finally out there.

"Yeah, we know!" Blake and Thomas said simultaneously.

"Oh, I guess Ella told you."

"Dude, we figured it out on your first day. Don't worry about it," Thomas said. "One of my older brothers wasn't good at sports either. He passed out, just like you, the first time my cousins made him play football at a family reunion. But after some coaching from some of his friends and tons of practice, he made the junior varsity team last fall."

"Wow, so how did he do?"

"He sat on the bench the whole season, but that's not the point."

"It isn't?"

"No. The point is he didn't give up. He made it through tryouts and wore the team jersey all season. He'll have another chance next year. In the meantime, he keeps practicing."

"Oh." I was still nervous. My heart rate accelerated as we made it to the field.

"The first thing you need to do is over-come your fear of the ball." Ella's tone was serious, but a slight smile appeared when she handed me the ball.

"What do you want me to do with it?"

"Kick it! Put it on the ground in front of you, then kick the ball to one of us. Give us a second to spread out." The three of them spread out across the field about twenty feet away from me. "Okay, kick it toward Blake first."

"Okay." I placed the ball on the ground and kicked it toward Blake. Instead of heading toward Blake, the ball headed for Ella. "Sorry."

"Don't apologize, just try it again." Ella kicked the ball back to me. I tried again, holding my breath the whole time. This time the ball made it to Blake.

"That's much better! Now kick it to me next," Ella said.

I kicked the ball toward Ella, but it stopped half-way. Ella ran and kicked the ball back to me for another try. The second time it headed straight for Ella. Next, I had to kick it to Thomas. I took a deep breath and gave the ball a swift kick. It headed directly to Thomas on the first try! For the first time in my life, I experienced a positive moment playing sports. We continued doing this for about twenty more minutes, and I was getting better each time.

"Let's try something different this time," Ella said, forming the time-out signal with her hands.

"What's next?" I asked.

"This time we're going to roll the ball to you, and you're going to kick it!" Ella sounded encouraging. "As the ball passes the halfway mark to you, start running toward it, and when it's in front of you, kick it!"

I did exactly what she said, but the result was a repeat of our last school practice. My feet fumbled over the ball, and I landed flat on the ground. Any confidence that I gained from the previous activity was now gone.

"Try it again, R.J."

"I can't do it, Ella!" A quiver could be heard in my voice, and my face burned from embarrassment.

"You can do it!" Blake and Thomas shouted back at me. I brushed the grass off my shirt and ran back to the starting spot. Ella gave me a thumbs up and waited for me to reciprocate. I took another deep breath and put up my thumb. She pulled back her arm and pitched the ball toward me. I started running when the ball passed the halfway mark. My foot made contact with the ball, but it just flew straight up in the air and back down. It landed only a few feet from where I kicked it. Another fail.

"R.J., that was awesome!" Ella shouted.

"That was horrible!"

"You hit the ball, dude! That's a start," added Thomas as the three made their way toward me. "We've got to go now. Ella's mom just pulled up."

"Thanks, guys! I really appreciate your help. See you tomorrow."

"Not if we see you first!" Blake said.

"That's so old, Blake!" Ella said laughing.

"See you in the morning, R.J."

The two jumped in the back seat of the car and waved goodbye to Blake and me as they pulled away. Blake gave me a fist bump and headed toward his apartment.

Walking back to our apartment, I felt a bit taller than before. Could some time practicing make me good at sports? I never had to practice music much. It just came naturally. I could hear a piece one time and then play it perfectly. But sports, that's a horse of a different color. Time would tell, I guess. There was only one problem. Time wasn't on my side. The kickball tournament was exactly three weeks away, and unless I planned to practice every waking moment, we were going to lose. And it would be all my fault!

CHAPTER SIXTEEN

NO BULLYING

I COULD HEAR THE alarm going off, but my body seemed unable to move. Every inch of it seemed to throb with pain. What have I done to myself? I've never felt this much pain after a good night's sleep. But did I actually have a good night's sleep? I remember watching the clock on my nightstand change from eight fifty-nine to nine o'clock. Then the next thing I remember is being awakened by the same clock's alarm, which is set for six a.m. That's nine hours! How could I feel more tired now than I did last night when I crawled into bed?

After some effort, I managed to hit the

snooze button and quickly drifted back to sleep, but it was short-lived. The extra nine minutes didn't seem to make any difference. Grabbing a change of clothes, I plodded to the small bathroom that Mallory and I shared and attempted to get ready. Maybe a hot shower would help loosen my muscles, because the current situation seemed hopeless. Just as I turned on the hot water, I heard a knock on the door.

"Hurry up, R.J.!" shouted Mallory.

"I just got in here!" I shouted back.

"According to my clock, you are running twenty minutes behind schedule, and I still need to do my hair."

"Okay. Okay. I'll try to hurry. Ouch!"

"What happened?"

"Nothing! My body hurts when the water hits it."

"Sore muscles will get you every time! Welcome to my world. It will get better soon. Now hurry up!"

"Okay. Okay!"

I tried my best to move quickly as I knew that Mallory was relentless when it came to getting into the bathroom. We each had our own bathroom in our real house, and I never had to rush. However, a few summers ago our family sublet a small apartment in Boston for an entire month, and Mallory and I had to share a bathroom. That part was bad, but the rest of the experience was phenomenal. Mallory attended a soccer camp while I participated in a three-week Master Class intensive at the Boston Conservatory at Berklee. We experienced all the sights and sounds of Boston as a family and despite our bathroom squabbles every morning and evening, Mallory and I enjoyed each other's company. She was and still is my biggest fan. But this morning, when I needed more time, she was not acting like my biggest fan. The knocks came every sixty seconds and didn't stop until I was out.

"It's about time! I'm going to be late because of you!"

"Now, Mallory, you'll have plenty of time," Mom said as she made her way to the kitchen.

"But, Mom, my hair is not cooperating this morning!"

"That's what happens when you go to bed with a wet head. I told you to dry it before going to sleep. Your hair is thick, and it has grown longer since school started in the fall. Looks like it might be time for a haircut."

"No way! Maybe a trim, but that's it."

"Now who's wasting time?" I asked, trying to shift some of the blame.

"I know what you're trying to do, and it won't work."

"Why don't you braid it for today? The forecast calls for warmer temperatures so that might be your best bet, especially if you have practice after school," Mom said.

"Shaving it off would help too!"

"Mom! Get him out of here before I have to regret what I'm going to do next!"

"Okay, I'm going."

"Why are you walking so slowly?" asked Mom.

"He's sore from using muscles that he never knew he had!"

"That's right. I saw Ella and two boys with you yesterday afternoon. Are all three in your class? They seem to enjoy your company."

"Yes. They seem pretty cool, even though none of them plays an instrument. I never thought I could make friends with someone if we didn't have music as a common interest."

"I'm sure Ella has a love for music, especially knowing about her sister. Dad, Mallory, and I can't play an instrument to save our lives, but we all love music."

"You make a valid point, Mom. I guess I never thought of it that way. I just assumed you all loved music because you love me."

"What's love got to do with it?" Mom looked at us with a cheeky smile.

"Huh?" Mallory asked.

"Never mind—I was thinking of a popular song when I was much younger."

"Tina Turner. Right?" I asked.

"Yes. How did you know?"

"Mom, I may play classical music, but I know music! Besides, my music teacher at Briarcliffe is a huge Tina Turner fan. He's been to at least twenty-five of her concerts."

"I guess that would qualify him as a big fan," Mom said, glancing at her watch. "We've got to get out of here, or we'll all be late!"

We made it to our destinations with time to spare. I walked into class just as the first bell was ringing and headed directly to my table. Sophie and Jennilee were reading quietly, but Andy's chair was still up.

"I guess Andy is running late today," I said to the two girls as I took down his chair.

"No, he's here," Jennilee responded. Sophie nodded in agreement.

"Oh, I thought ..."

"He's in the office talking with Assistant Principal Phillips," interrupted Sophie.

"Is he in trouble?"

"No," they answered in unison.

"So why is he in the assistant principal's office?"

"He's there because of you," Sophie answered.

"What? Am I in trouble?"

"No. He's just reporting something that happened before school," answered Jennilee.

"And it has to do with me?"

"Yes," Jennilee said, still staring down at her book.

"I'm so confused."

"Just tell him," Sophie said.

"No. Why don't you tell him?" Jennilee looked up crossly at Sophie.

"I wasn't the one who was there, so I think it should be you," Sophie said, returning the cross look.

"Oh, okay. Just don't get your feelings hurt, R.J. Do you promise?" she asked, looking me in the eyes.

"I promise I won't get my feelings hurt."

"This morning when Andy and I were

walking to class, three kids from Mrs. Granger's class were talking about you."

"Talking about me?"

"Maybe not talking about you—more like making fun of you. They said you were a loser and the only thing you could do well is pass out when you see a ball."

"Oh."

"They also called us losers for hanging out with you. Of course, we don't feel that way, R.J. I promise."

"Thank you. But I still don't understand why Andy went to see the assistant principal."

"He went to report the bullying. Mr. Phillips handles the discipline at our school, so that's why Andy's there."

"But won't it make it worse? The bully hates being tattled on. It will just escalate."

"Oh, you don't know Mr. Phillips. He's pretty serious about bullying. In fact, he and Mr. Bailey were part of a committee that focused on bullying. They spent a whole year attending conferences and creating programs at our school to tackle the bullying problem. Mr. Bailey started the RAK initiative for fifth grade when we were in third grade, and shortly after that Mr. Phillips, with the PTA board, painted the quote you see at the top of the fifth grade stairwell. Their hard work was very successful until these three students transferred here from another school in the district in January. They all ended up in Mrs. Granger's class, because she had the lowest numbers," Jennilee explained as the second bell rang.

"Good morning, boys and girls," Mr. Bailey said, walking to the board to update the date and goals for the day.

"Good morning, Mr. Bailey!" the class responded in unison.

"We'll talk more later," Jennilee whispered to me when we all stood to say the Pledge of Allegiance.

As we finished and began listening to the morning announcements, Andy slipped quietly into the room just as we were about to be seated. The three of us looked over at him in hopes of finding out how things went with Mr. Phillips. Andy just smiled and gave us all a quick nod. That was enough, at least for the moment. Mr. Bailey had a full day of activities and lessons for us, so our minds were too busy to dwell on any other thoughts.

By the time lunch rolled around we had completely forgotten about the whole incident.

NO BULLYING • 105

Later we found out that the three students in Mrs. Granger's class had been given in-school suspension.

Recess was still overwhelming, but I felt better when Thomas suggested that I shadow him out on the field. He wasn't pitching today. Instead, Blake was assigned the job. He did really well in getting the ball pitched smoothly along the slightly uneven ground. The recess whistle blew before I had my turn to kick, so overall Friday was the best day since I started at Fern Creek.

Mom had a few errands to do before we made it home that afternoon. As she pulled into our parking spot, I could see Ella, Thomas, and Blake waiting at the base of our apartment steps. Ella was holding the kickball and was the first up on her feet when she saw us get out of our car.

"Hey!" I called out, pushing the car door shut.

"Are you ready?" Ella asked.

"I think so."

"Would you kids like a grilled cheese sandwich in a few minutes?" Mom inquired as we all gathered at the base of the steps.

"Sure, Mrs. Baker! That would be great,"

Ella responded, handing the ball to Thomas.

"Yes, it would be awesome," Thomas added.

Before Mom had unlocked the apartment door, the four of us were already on the field. We practiced, took a short break and ate the sandwiches Mom brought out to us, then practiced for another two hours before Ella's mom arrived to pick up her and Thomas. Blake and I continued practicing until my legs couldn't take any more. Truthfully, I was really tired, but my confidence was growing stronger. My fear of the ball was almost gone; I just needed to work on running and kicking at the same time. If only that could be as easy as learning a new sonata.

CHAPTER SEVENTEEN

ELLA'S IDEA

THE FOUR OF US continued to practice every afternoon for the next five days. I could tell that my body was getting used to this new routine as the soreness was almost nonexistent. I knew I was getting better, but I still couldn't kick the ball far enough to make a base hit. Nothing seemed to help until Thursday afternoon when Ella showed up at my door all by herself.

"Where are Thomas and Blake?" I asked, scanning down the steps to see if they were there.

"They both have family plans this evening, so they can't make it today. Besides, I have something I want to share with you that I think will help your game."

"Oh, okay. Do you want something to drink?" I asked, trying to be polite.

"No, I'm good for now. Let's head down to the field, and I'll share my idea with you."

We started walking toward the field. Before long, we were racing each other to see who would get there first. Ella nearly beat me, but I nudged ahead just as we stepped onto the grassy area.

"Not bad, Mr. Baker. You nearly beat me!"

"Hey, I did beat you!"

"Almost!"

"Are you blind?"

"No, but you're rude! Are you ready to hear my idea?" she asked.

"Okay, but for the record, I won the race!" I boasted.

"Whatever! If it's that important, I'll let you believe the lie."

"Lie? What?"

"I'm just kidding! You won, but just barely. There, is that better? Can I share my idea now?"

"Okay, now that you've accepted your loss, I'll listen."

"Sheesh! You're so competitive!" Ella laughed.

"So, what's your big idea?" I was eager to hear what she had to say.

"I know we're not supposed to talk about it—but you know how much you love music?"

"Yeah ..."

"Running and kicking the ball is similar to music."

"Are you feeling okay?"

"No, really."

"How?"

"Let me explain."

"Go right ahead. I can't wait to hear how you connect the two."

"Music has rhythm."

"And ..."

"That's it. The connection is the rhythm. When the ball is pitched, a rhythm is created."

"Okay, and ..."

"If you can feel the rhythm and move in sync as you're running toward the ball to kick it, the result will be a home run. I just know it! Are you willing to try?"

"I guess."

"You don't sound too sure. I've thought about this all week, and I know this is the key to your success and our class winning the tournament! Just try it! You've got nothing to lose."

"I have already made a fool of myself countless times, so I guess there's not much more of my pride to lose."

"Are all musicians this dramatic?"

"Huh?"

"Never mind. I'll pitch and you watch for the rhythm."

"Okay, but I don't think—"

"Don't think, just do!"

Ella pitched the ball, and I watched the rhythm it created as it travelled across the grass. As the ball passed the center point, I began running toward the ball following the same rhythm. Thrusting my right foot forward, it made a direct impact with the ball, causing it to soar across the field with great force.

"You did it, R.J.! I knew it would work!"

"You were right, Ella! I can't believe I just did that! That felt amazing!"

"Hey, R.J.! That was awesome!" Mallory shouted, running onto the field. "I'm so impressed! I would love to see it again, but we've got to go. Mom needs for you to come home."

"Just one more, Mal, please?"

"You know I would like nothing more, but it's really important."

"But Ella is—"

"Don't worry about me, R.J. I'll just call my mom. She can be here in a few minutes. She's only up the road visiting with a friend. I can join her."

"Are you sure?"

"Yes, no problem."

"See you tomorrow, and thanks so much!"

"You've got it."

"I really mean it—thank you!"

"If you taught him how to kick like that, then I thank you too!" Mallory added as we waved bye and headed back to the apartment. Ella gave us a two-thumbs-up sign and called her mom.

Walking up the stairs, all the excitement from the last thirty minutes faded. No matter what strides I had made in the last two weeks, this life was a facade, and Dad was still not with us. Was he safe? Would he be joining us soon? Did he miss us? We were quickly approaching the two week mark since that horrible evening and those answers seemed so far away at the moment. Maybe Mom had some positive news to share with us. Doubt was quickly becoming a constant presence, and I was not fond of this current relationship. I needed to know something definite about Dad's status before I could enjoy anything this temporary life had to offer.

CHAPTER EIGHTEEN

A CALL FROM MARSHAL STEVENS

MOM HAD US SIT on the small sofa in the living room, while she sat in a chair across from us. She was holding an unfamiliar cell phone in her hand. It wasn't the pay-as-you-go cell phone that she picked up that Saturday afternoon before moving into this apartment. This was some type of special phone. She clasped it tightly and pursed her lips before talking. My fear grew with each passing second, and I didn't know if I cared to hear the news she was about to share. I had managed to collect more dread-filled moments in the last two weeks than I've had in my entire existence of ten years, eight months, and fourteen days. I could tell that Mallory was feeling unhinged. She only picked at her fingers when she was nervous, and from where I was sitting, I could see her doing that now.

"I had a call from Marshal Stevens shortly after I got home."

"Is Dad okay?" Mallory asked, jumping to her feet.

"Honey, he's fine. Have a seat so I can share the details."

Mallory sat back down, but this time she sat closer to me, putting her arm around my shoulders. Her gesture was surprisingly comforting, and for a moment, I felt my heartbeat settle down. Mom smiled at us for a second then continued talking.

"Your Dad has been working undercover with the FBI for almost three weeks. I think he might have mentioned to one of you that he was thinking of resigning from his job ..."

"Yes, he hinted about it to me on our way home from a soccer practice," Mallory interrupted.

"That very next day he was approached at work by one of the clinical staff who was actually an undercover agent. Apparently, the

FBI has been keeping a close watch on a group of new investors at the company for the last ten months. The undercover agent asked your dad if he would be willing to wear a wire for an entire week."

"A wire?" I asked, not understanding what she meant.

"A hidden microphone that records conversations," Mallory explained.

"Oh, I get it. Cool! Go on, Mom."

"Dad wore the wire and participated in a series of discussions with the investors and company officers. It appears that the investors were laundering money from a questionable overseas account. They needed the drug that Dad's department was working on to hit the market immediately so that the FDA wouldn't question the surplus of money. Several times throughout the conversations, the investors threatened to ruin Dad if he didn't change the trial results in favor of bringing the drug to market. Each conversation was heard and recorded by the surveillance team.

The FBI feels certain that this evidence will be enough to convict the investors and the company officers conspiring with them and put them away for a very long time. Large sums of illegal money belonging to some bad people are at stake, so for our safety, we were put in this witness protection program. If these people were to find out that Dad conspired with the FBI, our lives and his would be at risk. All of this resulted in the U.S. Marshals showing up at our door that Friday. We must be cautious not to give away our identities. We must continue life as the Baker family and no one, I mean absolutely no one, can know these details. Do you understand?"

"Yes," we answered simultaneously.

"But where is Dad now?" I asked.

"Dad is safe. He is with the FBI and will remain in his own protective custody until the Superior Court hearing on May 17th."

I interrupted, "Does this mean Dad is a hero?"

"Yes, I believe this definitely puts your dad in hero status."

"Wow! This is unbelievable!" exclaimed Mallory.

"Let's not get ahead of ourselves just yet. Dad needs to testify in court and then there needs to be a conviction."

"Oh, they're going down!" I announced, jumping up in excitement.

"Now, more than ever, we need to maintain a low profile. We must remain calm and keep life at our new status quo. Once this is behind us, we can return to our home and pick up where we left off."

"Do you think Carnegie Hall will happen?" I asked, even though I already knew the answer.

"Honey, the Carnegie Hall event is only a few weeks away, and even fast-tracked trials like this one take time. There's always next year."

"That's what I thought, but I guess I was hoping the answer would somehow be different now that there is a court date."

"Superior Court cases rarely finish in less than two weeks. They need to select a jury and that alone could take a few days."

"I get it. You're right; there's always next year." I could feel my emotions well up inside me, but I managed not to cry. After all, our family's safety was more important than playing at Carnegie Hall. Mom took a moment to compose herself before preparing dinner. We all rallied to the kitchen.

"Who's in the mood for homemade pizza with all the toppings?" Mom asked.

"That sounds awesome!" Mallory shouted from across the room. "Would you like some help?"

"If you're offering, I accept!" exclaimed Mom.

"I can help too, Mom," I added, opening a drawer and pulling out three aprons.

"Many hands make less work, and I never refuse help. Just make sure you wash your hands. I've got standards to maintain," Mom announced, giving Mallory and me a haughty look that made us laugh.

Considering the events of this entire day, I think it was the first time I felt like we were the Bakers. Yes, Dad wasn't part of the scenario, but somehow knowing that he would soon be declared a hero, I didn't mind as much. For the time being, Dad was away on business, and I could live with that.

CHAPTER NINETEEN

NOTHING TO FEAR

WE SPENT THE WEEKEND still processing the news about Dad. During breakfast on Saturday morning, Mom offered one more detail that added a whole new layer of complicated to an already difficult situation. Due to the nature of the case, the possibility of a televised court case was likely. Dad would be on TV, and we had to pretend that we didn't know him. People would be talking about the case, and we had to act oblivious to any of details.

While I was lying on my bed, a variety of scenarios played in my head. What if Ella recognized Dad? He only made it to part of the October performance due to work, but he was normally a regular attendee with an above average applause. Let's just say he was the ring leader of my cheering section. Mallory was always embarrassed, especially when she brought a friend. I could not understand why it didn't bother her when Dad cheered during a soccer game. I guess being cheered for is less embarrassing than having people turn to see who is cheering—and you're sitting right beside the culprit.

Until recently, I never would have categorized my life as complicated. School came easy, and music was my heartbeat. Life was organic—everything felt and occurred naturally. My current life was far from organic; synthetic is more like it. It was manufactured. With a low-heat threshold. Sheesh. The quote above Mr. Bailey's door raced through my thoughts. "The only thing we have to fear is fear itself." What is that actually supposed to mean?

My fears are based on so many unknowns. It's the unknowns and the "what ifs" that I fear the most. I wonder if President Roosevelt would have been able to see that my situation went beyond his ten words. If he had known the details of my current circumstances, maybe he would have spoken more comforting words. My only solace is knowing that this synthetic life will be over soon. I just have to survive until then.

CHAPTER TWENTY

TOO CLOSE FOR COMFORT

ENTERING THE FIFTH GRADE stairwell on Monday morning, I came face-to-face with one of the bullies in Mrs. Granger's class. I heard other students call him Ty, which I think is short for Tyler. For a second I froze, but then something came over me because before I could think it through, I said, "Hey, Ty!" For a few seconds he stared right through me. Then he grabbed my lunch bag and tossed it in the trash as he continued walking. I heard him mumble "loser" under his breath. The in-school suspension hadn't changed a thing. I slowed my pace to wait for the hall to clear before I pulled my lunch out of the trash. Luckily, there wasn't much in the trash yet, so my bag wasn't soiled, just a little crushed. Walking into class, Andy noticed something was bothering me.

"Hey, are you okay?"

"Yeah," I answered, trying to make it sound believable.

"Did something happen in the hallway?"

"No, I'm fine." He wasn't buying what I was trying to sell.

"I don't believe you. Was it one of the bullies?"

"It's nothing. Really. I'm just a little tired from the weekend."

"Are you sure?"

"Yeah, we had a bunch of chores to do. My mom had a mile-long list."

"Spring cleaning frenzy, that's what my mom calls it."

"Yep."

"We got home late from visiting my aunt, uncle, and two cousins. They live about two hours from here, and we only get to see them every other month. My aunt and uncle have the coolest house. They live on fifty acres and breed Shetland ponies. We didn't get to ride any this trip as they were hired for a local carnival," Andy said.

"That's cool! The closest I've ever come to riding a horse or pony was on the merry-go-round at a theme park."

"That's the only horse my mom will ever ride. It's hard to believe that my aunt is her sister. They're so different. My mom is definitely the better cook. She usually ends up cooking dinner while my aunt bakes chocolate fudge brownies and my all-time favorite—snickerdoodles."

"Those are my sister's favorite," I said just as the second bell rang. We all stood up for the Pledge. Once the announcements were completed, Mr. Bailey had us gather for our morning meeting. He started the day's meeting by reading a quote.

> *Carry out a random act of kindness, with no expectation of reward, safe in the knowledge that one day someone might do the same for you.*

Mr. Bailey paused before rereading it. "'Carry out a random act of kindness, with no expectation of reward, safe in the knowledge that one day someone might do the same for you.' Does anyone know who originally spoke those words?"

"Was it someone famous?" asked Charlie, forgetting to raise his hand.

"Did I see a raised hand, Mr. Reynolds?" Mr. Bailey sounded serious, but a faint smile appeared on his face.

"Oops, sorry, Mr. Bailey. I guess my curiosity got the best of me."

"I can tell, Charlie. And yes, the person who originally spoke these words was famous." This time Charlie raised his hand.

"You used the word *was* instead of *is*, so my guess is that it's a famous person who's no longer alive. Am I right?"

"You're on the right track. Any guesses?"

"Manhattan Gandhi?"

A few giggles surfaced from the group. Mr. Bailey did his best to hold in his laugh.

"Charlie, it's Ma-hat-ma Gandhi."

"So … am I right?"

"No, but it was a really good try. It was actually Princess Diana."

"You mean Prince Harry's mom?" Charlie asked.

"Yes, Prince Harry's mom, or as the British would say 'mum.' Now, who can tell me, in your own words, what it means?" He waited a few seconds then scanned the group and called on Ella.

"I think it means that we should do a random act of kindness just because it's the right thing to do, not because we might get noticed or receive a compliment. And then maybe the people who receive these random acts of kindness will pay it forward and someday, when you really need it, someone will do a random act of kindness for you." Ella's response received a spontaneous round of applause and a smile from Mr. Bailey.

"Ella, I couldn't have explained it better myself. Thank you for sharing, and thank you, boys and girls, for acknowledging Ella's brilliant explanation. Before I forget, I need to remind those of you who haven't already done so to make sure you complete the RAK initiative and post it on the website. Our deadline is quickly approaching."

Mr. Bailey leaned a bit forward, and his expression suddenly became serious before he continued. "It's come to my attention that some of you have experienced some bullying lately. As a class, we have created a safe and accepting environment. Overall, our school has made great strides in eliminating bullying. However, that doesn't mean we won't be challenged now and then. As always, every adult in this school is dedicated to supporting the zero tolerance for bullying. But we need your help. Reporting bullying incidences in a timely manner is the primary way you can help us eliminate bullying. On Friday, Andy reported an incident that happened before school, and Mr. Philips handled it immediately."

Mr. Bailey's words stirred up emotions from the morning encounter with Ty, and I knew I had to say something. As I raised my hand, I could feel my face turn red.

"Yes, Mr. Baker. Do you have a question?"

"No, it's not a question. I think I need to report a bullying incident."

"Sure. Give me a few seconds to get the class started on an activity, and then we can chat."

I nodded my head and walked over to Mr. Bailey's desk, where I waited quietly for him to finish. Mr. Bailey introduced and explained each reading activity before assigning groups. I listened so I would know what to do when I got back to my group. He had some interesting assignments planned, and I was eager to start. Walking back to his desk, Mr. Bailey patted my shoulder and said, "I'm so proud of you, R.J. You're new here, and I'm still getting to know you, but I'm glad you feel comfortable enough to share your experience with bullying."

"Thank you, Mr. Bailey. I wasn't sure about this until our morning meeting. It happened on my way to class. Well, it's actually happened before, but I didn't report it. It was my first week here, so I wasn't sure."

"No worries, R.J. I completely understand. Please, go on."

"This morning, I came face-to-face with Ty, I mean Tyler in Mrs. Granger's class, and said hi. I'm not really sure why I said hi. It just came out. He was one of the three students who made fun of me that first week of school. Tyler stared at me, then grabbed my lunch bag from my hand and threw it in the trash. As he walked away, I heard him call me a loser. That's what the three of them have been calling me ever since I passed out on the field."

"I am proud of your bravery, R.J. Your teammates have already shared some of the details from your first week, and I was hoping that it was just an isolated incidence. However, after Andy's encounter on Friday, I knew we had to address this further. Mrs. Granger and

I will have a chat during specials. This will be stopped, I promise."

"Thank you, Mr. Bailey. I guess I'd better get started on my work."

"Sure thing."

I was hoping Mr. Bailey's promise would hold true. The more I got to know him, the more I liked him as a teacher. He would definitely fit right in at The Briarcliffe School for the Performing Arts. Somehow, even though I did not doubt Mr. Bailey would do his best to fix the problem, I knew that I had to do something myself. Maybe a random act of kindness with no expectation of reward was just the thing I needed to do to win over these students. I thought about it more during specials and lunch, but nothing was coming to mind. I couldn't give up that easily. If Dad was brave enough to wear a wire and cooperate with the FBI to take down some pretty shady people, the least I could do is think of some random acts of kindness that would defuse my bullies.

CHAPTER TWENTY-ONE

THE SUBSTITUTE

AS MALLORY AND I were cleaning up the breakfast dishes, the meteorologist on one of the local news channels was rambling on about how our area had record rains this week. The last time I saw rains like this was when we were vacationing at Disney World in Florida. A tropical storm had stalled over the state and although the winds weren't that bad, the rain came down by the bucket for days! Most of the local people acted like it was normal, but Mallory and I were freaked out. We wore transparent ponchos Mom had picked up at one of the convenience stores. They helped some, but our feet were soaked. The skin on my toes was wrinkled like a prune the whole trip. Dad said Floridians were used to heavy downpours, and so long as the winds were light, they went about their business as usual.

If I had to compare, the rain here wasn't as bad as the rain we had experienced in Florida, but it was enough to flood the school playground and shut down recess for the week. Part of me was thrilled to skip recess, but the other part was eager to practice my kicking. I know I am getting better, but Ella, Thomas, and Blake wanted me to keep my improvement a secret. They thought it would be cool to surprise the rest of the class.

Unfortunately, the rain also kept the four of us from practicing much after school. We managed to get in twenty minutes of practice on Wednesday, but the slick grass made it hard to keep our footing. At one point, we all were face-down in the grass laughing our heads off. It was the most fun I've had in a while. Laughing and rolling in wet grass was something I would have avoided in the past. But I must admit, there was something about it that made me feel free, just like when I play the cello.

All week long I had been thinking about

an act of kindness that I could do for Ty and his sidekicks. Now it was Friday morning and still nothing. This was going to be really hard. I wanted to leave the random part out since I had an ulterior motive to stop the bullying. It was becoming evident that I needed a Plan B, whatever that might be. I could hear Mom coming down the hall. Grabbing three umbrellas from the hall closet, Mom handed one to Mallory and one to me, and we were out the door and on our way to school. Today was three weeks since this whole synthetic life started. Hopefully, it will also be remembered as the halfway point to it being a thing of the past.

When I entered the fifth grade hall, I could hear students whispering and pointing toward my classroom door. I wondered why they were acting so strangely. My answer came as soon as I entered the room. We had a substitute. At least I think she was a substitute. It was hard to tell. I've never seen a substitute like her before. She had long pink hair and her clothes looked like a mash-up of the Victorian and Old West times. She was a walking piece of art.

"Wow, she's definitely rocking that Steam Punk look!" Sophie said as she unloaded her backpack.

"Oh, so that's what it's called," Jennilee said.

"Does anyone know her name?" Andy asked.

"No, but Leigh from Mrs. Hamilton's class said that her sister had her as a sub in middle school," said Jennilee.

By the time the second bell rang, the whole class was sitting wide-eyed, waiting to hear the sub's name. And then she spoke. Her accent was definitely British.

"Hello, class. My name is Ms. Marigold Merriweather-Simmons of Sussex, England, but you may call me Ms. Simmons."

"Good morning, Ms. Simmons!" The whole class responded in unison, almost as if in a trance. Class with Ms. Simmons was an experience. Her accent made everything sound intriguing, and you couldn't help but notice something new every time you looked at her.

Shortly after guided reading, Ms. Simmons walked to the front of the room and stood quietly for a few minutes waiting for everyone's attention. It looked as if she was ready to begin a performance of some sort, but instead she shared a quote.

Do not underestimate a moment of your kindness. It has the power to change lives in ways you may never know.

Her accent made each word seem a bit more important and the message more profound, at least for me. "Your teacher, Mr. Bailey, left a message in his sub plans to share a quote about Random Acts of Kindness. I chose this one as it is one that resonates deep within the fiber of my being." At this point, you could have heard a pin drop as we all wondered what she meant. A hand went up in the front of the room.

"Thank you for raising your hand, young lady. What is your question?" Ms. Simmons asked Angelica, who normally didn't participate in class discussions.

"Why does it resonate deep within your fibers? Does it have something to do with your clothes?" Angelica asked, looking a bit confused.

"Not the fibers of my clothes, dear. I meant that this quote spoke to me because long ago someone just like you took a moment to share a Random Act of Kindness with me. That moment changed my life forever. That girl had no idea how much her kindness meant to me in that moment. Likewise, you may never know how much your kindness will mean to someone you encounter. It could be today or someday in the future, but your kindness can change a life. Always be ready to spread a bit of kindness in the world. It can make the difference between an ordinary day and an extraordinary one. Does that make sense now, love?"

"Yes, thank you, Ms. Simmons! I get it now," Angelica answered enthusiastically.

"Now, everyone, please take out your math homework so we can review it together. It appears that Mr. Bailey will be giving you a test on Monday instead of today." A sigh of relief was heard across the room, and we all pulled out our math homework from our homework folders. Though I think most of the students felt ready for the math test, a few extra days still was a welcome surprise.

"Is there someone who wouldn't mind leading homework review?" Ms. Simmons asked, scanning the room.

"R.J. can do it!" Jennilee called out before raising her hand.

"Are you keen to do it, R.J.?"

"Me? Sure, I guess so, Ms. Simmons," I answered. I was a solid math student and enough time had passed for me to feel comfortable around my peers. I walked to the front of the room and began to review the fraction to decimal conversions. It felt pretty good to take the lead in my new surroundings, and for the moment, I forgot that my life was altered. Finishing the final problem, I walked by Ms. Simmons and asked her a quick question.

"Ms. Simmons, may I go to the restroom?"

"Yes, R.J., and thank you for a brilliant review of last night's math homework!"

"You're welcome, Ms. Simmons. It was nothing."

"I sense there's more to you than meets the eye, R.J."

"I'm just an ordinary fifth grader," I answered, trying not to sound nervous.

"For some reason, ordinary is not a word I would choose to describe you, love."

"I really need to use the bathroom," I said, hoping I could curtail this uncomfortable conversation.

"Yes, by all means, please go."

That was a relief. With the court case looming in the near future, I didn't want anyone trying to see my true identity. When I entered the boys' bathroom, I could hear faint sounds of someone crying in one of the stalls. I hesitated for a second then walked over to the stall door and asked, "Are you okay? Should I call someone?"

"No. Just leave." The voice seemed weak but familiar. I started to walk away, but the quote that Ms. Simmons shared flooded my mind, and I knocked lightly on the stall door.

"I said leave!"

"No," I responded. "Let me help you, please."

"You can't help me! Just get out!"

"Maybe if you tell me what's wrong, I could help you."

"*Maybe if you tell me what's wrong, I could help you*," the voice mocked. "Right!"

"Try me."

"It's nothing. My dad just bailed on me again," he said bitterly.

"Are your parents ..."

"Divorced! My dad was supposed to take me camping for my birthday this weekend. He promised that he would the last time he cancelled!"

"This is your birthday weekend?"

"Yeah! It's already ruined," he answered.

"I get how you're feeling."

"Yeah? And how would *you* know?"

"Well, I haven't seen my dad in a while."

"Are your parents divorced?"

"No," I answered.

"So, why haven't you seen your dad?"

"It's complicated."

"When is he coming home?"

"I'm not sure when, but I know he will."

"Yeah, well, good for you. How does that help me?" he said sarcastically.

"I know it doesn't help you, but I get how you're feeling right now." At this point, I was pretty sure I was talking to Ty.

"Riiight, sure you do!"

"No, really, I kinda do. It's hard, but you just need to keep a positive outlook."

"Hey, who are you?"

"It's ..." I paused until I mustered the courage to continue, "R.J."

"What? Are you kidding me? Get out of here and leave me alone!"

"But I really need to pee!" I said.

"Go downstairs to another bathroom!"

"I won't make it. Please, I really need to go!"

"Fine! You better not say anything!"

"About what?" I tried to sound like I had

no idea what he was talking about.

"Just do your business and get out!"

I ran into the farthest stall, closed the door, and took a deep breath before relieving myself. After a few seconds, I could hear someone enter the bathroom.

"Ty!" a voice called out.

"Yeah!" Ty answered, trying to mask his emotions.

"Mrs. Granger sent me to check on you. We're about to start the test. Are you coming?" I recognized the voice. It was one of Ty's buddies, one of the ones who laughed at me on the bus.

"What's her problem? Tell her I'll be there in a minute and get out!"

"Okay, okay! You're sure in a bad mood today!"

"Whatever! Just go!"

I could hear him leave. Ty let out a big sigh before opening the stall and walking to the sinks. By the time I made it to the sinks, Ty was drying his face with a paper towel. I looked straight ahead and didn't say a word. As Ty walked out, I whispered, "I forgive you."

Ty stopped dead in his tracks. He stood there for a second, clenching his left fist. I thought he was going to hit me or at least call me a loser or something. Instead, he took a deep breath and walked out the door, never once turning his head.

I waited a couple of minutes to let him get down the hall. A trickle of sweat slid down my back, and I could feel my muscles relax. I had confronted my bully with kindness. All week long I had been thinking of a way to be kind to him. Never in my wildest dreams did I think it would happen like this. I'm not sure if it will fix anything for either of us, but at least I had faced one of my fears, and that has to count for something.

CHAPTER TWENTY-TWO

A WORLD FULL OF QUIRKY PEOPLE

THE SKY REMAINED OVERCAST until late Saturday afternoon when a patch of blue streaked with hues of purple, red, and orange appeared in the distance. From the balcony directly outside our small family room, I could see puddles of water begin to evaporate. Hopefully, Ella and I could continue working on my kicking skills and then move on to throwing and catching. I was content for the moment to sit in the damp wicker chair recollecting yesterday's events. I still couldn't get over my encounter with Ty. Somehow it felt like a scene from an inspirational movie.

Right about now I would give anything for this whole thing to be part of a movie script. On the other hand, I feel like pretending to be R.J. and living in his world has helped me grow in ways that being Preston never would have.

I smiled as I thought about our sub, Ms. Simmons. She will never know how much her words affected the outcome of my week. She was definitely different but in a good, quirky way. Being called a prodigy cellist since the age of four never seemed that different from the kids I was surrounded by at The Briarcliffe School for the Performing Arts. I wonder how long it would have taken me to realize that I am different, even quirky in my own way, if I was still at that school.

From what I can tell so far, being quirky isn't as peculiar as it might sound. In some ways, we are all quirky. I thought about it. Some of us are obsessed with video games, some with sports, or some reading. We dress differently, like our fries plain, drenched with ketchup or ranch dressing, or—as absurd as it might sound—don't even like fries at all. Some of us love action adventure movies, some love sci-fi trilogies or Disney movies, or even horror flicks.

Our tastes in music range from heavy metal to opera. Let's face it; our world is full of quirky people doing life together. So, if we're all quirky, why do we still have bullies?

The only explanation I can figure is that bullies are scared to let others see their hurts or weaknesses. Ty was my example. He bullied me because he was hurting. Ty's dad let him down repeatedly, and that made Ty lash out at other people. All of us can experience hurt, fear, and weakness. Heck, I suffered all three during my first day at Fern Creek Elementary. We all experience hurt or fear sometime. Mom and Dad have always told my sister and me that life is the best teacher. I never really understood what they meant until now.

The slider opened, and Mom stepped out onto the balcony.

"Look at that sky," she said, taking a seat beside me. "Dinner is just about ready. Maybe we could have our meal out here tonight."

"Sounds like a great idea, Mom! I can help with the set up."

"Okay. Hey, you looked like you were deep in thought when I came out here. What were you thinking about?"

"I was just thinking how we're all quirky in some way."

"Quirky? You think I'm quirky?"

"Uh … yeah, I mean … yes, I think sometimes you are quirky."

"Hmm … I guess you're right. I can't get enough of carpet and paint samples. I've been having mental withdrawal pains ever since this new life took over."

"You're definitely weird."

"Don't push it, kiddo! Remember, I'm the one who feeds you around here."

"And for that, I'm very thankful! Can we eat now?"

"You get that card table out of the closet and set it up out here. I'll grab the plates and such."

"I'm on it!"

"Ask Mallory to help. She's cleaning up her room."

"Mallory!" I shouted across the living room.

"I could have done that!"

"Sorry, just thought I'd save some time. My stomach's growling!"

"Mallory!" Mom shouted, looking in the direction of the bedrooms.

"Huh? I thought you—"

"I'm just showing off my quirkiness!"

I just shook my head. "Awww! Like mother, like son."

"Wouldn't want to disappoint."

As always, Mom's cooking didn't disappoint. We watched the sunset, cleaned up our mess, and went inside to finish off the evening with a movie. The only thing missing was Dad. I wondered what he was thinking about tonight.

CHAPTER TWENTY-THREE

SUNDAY AFTERNOON FUN

THE WEEKEND FLEW BY. Ella appeared on Sunday with Thomas as expected, and we practiced for nearly three hours. Blake joined in when he and his parents got home from church. He was dressed in some new khakis and a royal blue polo, so he went inside to change before running onto the field. The grass was still a bit damp, but not enough to cause any slipping. After I missed catching the ball too many times, I had an idea. I started thinking of the ball as the bow for my cello. I would never want to drop my bow for fear of damaging it. Once I locked this image in my head, my stats changed.

I caught the ball more often than not, no matter who threw it to me or who kicked it in my direction. Blake, Ella, and Thomas made a big deal about my improvement. That made me feel good and even a little proud. I was pretty bad the first day we started practicing, but now I was definitely better than bad. Not an expert by any means, just better.

"Looking good, R.J.!" Mallory shouted, approaching the field.

"Our chances of winning the kickball tournament have seriously improved!" Ella added as Mallory gave each of them a fist bump.

"Do you want to join in?" Thomas asked Mallory.

"Sure, I thought you'd never ask!" Mallory answered.

"Hey, can you use another player?" It was Mom. She appeared at the edge of the grassy area wearing Dad's hoodie.

"Sure, Mrs. Baker," Ella responded.

"I just had a great idea!" Blake said. "I can ask my mom, dad, and sister if they would like to join us. We can almost have a real game!"

"Cool!" Thomas said. "I'm going to call Mom and ask her if she and Dad would like to join us."

"Okay, but hurry before it gets too late," Ella said. "Have your mom call my family too!"

"Will do!"

In less than twenty-five minutes thirteen players were divided into two teams of six, with Thomas volunteering to be the pitcher for both sides. Ella's sister, Natalia, brought her multicolored pom-poms and cheered from the sidelines. My team was out on the field first. Typically, my heart would be pounding at the very thought of a team sport activity, but my heartbeat was surprisingly normal. I smiled at Ella as I raced toward my assigned spot on the field. The next few hours were as close to perfect as one could get considering everything my family was facing. Dad would definitely get along with the other dads. For now, I just had to imagine that Dad was okay, or I would lose it. I've come too far to break down now.

CHAPTER TWENTY-FOUR

A MOMENT OF WEAKNESS

"SO, YOU THINK THAT Ty will stop bullying you now?" Sophie asked me during lunch on Monday.

"I'm not really sure. He had the opportunity to call me a loser or even hit me as he left the bathroom, but he didn't. That's got to count for something," I answered and took a rather large bite from my sandwich.

"I'm not sold!" Jennilee objected.

"Why?" Andy asked.

"A kid like that doesn't just stop being a bully. The three of you are so gullible. Reality is—he's still a bully, but now you have ammunition," she said, raising both eyebrows and pursing her lips.

I finally managed to swallow my bite. Jennilee was definitely wrong and for the first time since I met her, I was disappointed. "Why would I use what happened as ammunition? I'm better than that. You're better than that!"

"The bullied never have a chance for revenge. We have to forgive and let it go. How is that fair? When do we get our turn to see the bullies hurt as much as they have hurt their victims? We're always told we need to take the high road. I bet the person who came up with that was never bullied!" Jennilee's face had turned beet red, and her breathing became labored.

"Hey, calm down, Jennilee. This is not like you. You don't want to trigger your asthma." Sophie spoke calmly, placing both hands on Jennilee's shoulders.

"Sophie's right, Jennilee. You're working yourself into a full-blown asthma attack," Andy added.

"No, I'll be fine. I don't understand why you don't see this as an opportunity to stop the bullying. Catching Ty slobbering behind the bathroom stall, why it's practically priceless!"

Jennilee's breathing became less labored, but her face was still red.

"'You are not better than anyone else, but no one is better than you.' Isn't that what we see each morning when we walk into the fifth grade hallway?" I asked Jennilee, hoping she would calm down. "You don't stop a bully by being a bully. We all matter. At least I hope we do. Isn't that the whole reason Mr. Bailey started the RAK initiative?"

"But now that you know Ty's weakness, R.J. ..."

"I only told you guys because I thought I could trust you!"

"Hey, don't put us all in the same category!" Andy inserted, while Sophie nodded in agreement.

"Okay! Okay! You're right. Don't cast me aside!" pleaded Jennilee.

"That was scary. I hope we never see that side of you again," Sophie said to her.

"Sorry, I had a weak moment! I promise that's all it was! I do know better. Really."

"I believe you, Jennilee. It just caught us off guard. But just to be sure—you promise to keep what I told you a secret?" I looked directly at her to make sure her response was sincere.

"Yes. Yes, I promise. Sorry, I didn't mean for you to lose your trust in me," Jennilee said, displaying a pleading smile. Her face was no longer red, and she was now breathing normally.

"No worries. We're good. Besides, we've got to focus on the tournament. It's only a few days away!" Andy said, putting out a fist bump. Jennilee returned it, and we all went back to eating our lunches in peace.

CHAPTER TWENTY-FIVE

YOUR FACE TELLS ME OTHERWISE

AFTER SCHOOL ON MONDAY, I was greeted outside my apartment door by Ella who was holding a worn cello case. She was a tad winded from carrying the large instrument up the stairs but was determined to get out her words before I could say anything.

"Okay, so I know you said you were taking a break from playing, but I discussed it with my mom and dad last night, and we all agreed that your talent is too amazing to just take a break! One of my neighbors, Mrs. Monahan, is a retired anthropologist, okay, I don't know exactly what that is, but she also was a "splendid cellist in her day"—her words, not mine. When I told her that I had a talented friend currently without his cello, she was more than happy to lend me, or you, her cello. All she asked is that you play for her one afternoon. Here you go. I can't stay today because Mom set up a hair appointment for my sister and me."

"I don't know what to say."

"Thank you would be fine."

"But how did you know that I didn't have my cello?"

"I just knew. Well, I figured it out the day Mrs. Wells introduced the stringed instruments. For a musical prodigy, your expression seemed distant. I wondered about it all night long and finally concluded that only a person who lost something would look that way. You don't have to give me any details, just play. I've got to go. Mom's waiting. See you tomorrow!"

Ella dashed down the steps and got into her mom's car. I waved and hollered out a thank you as the car drove off.

As I held the cello case, I was overwhelmed by uncontrollable emotion. I stepped back into the apartment and closed the door before actually letting it all out. It was ugly, no other way to describe it. Up until this moment, I had managed to suppress most of these feelings. But knowing that a cello was this close was just too hard. I wanted to open the case and start playing, but decided I'd better wait to ask Mom first. She had dropped me off before heading to the market to pick up stuff for dinner. The next twenty minutes seemed to drag on for an eternity. Would she let me play, or would I have to hide the cello in the hall closet? The answer couldn't come soon enough. I went to wash my face as I knew it would be all blotchy.

Mom walked in the door just as I was drying my face. I could hear her keys jingle as she dropped them on the counter with the grocery bags. "R.J., are you here?" Mom called out from the kitchen.

"Yes, I'll be right there!" I shouted back from the bathroom, examining my face in the mirror for any remaining blotchiness.

"I expected to see you playing kickball with your friends when I pulled into the parking lot. Is everything okay?"

"Yeah, Ella had to get a haircut today," I said as I walked into the kitchen.

"Why is the front of your hair all wet?" Mom asked.

"Oh, I just washed my face. I felt a little overheated." I answered.

"Overheated? It's not that warm outside. Are you sure you're feeling okay?"

"Yeah, I guess."

"Did something happen at school again? Was it that Ty kid?" asked Mom.

"No, nothing like that."

"Your face looks swollen. What are you not telling me?" probed Mom.

"You always know. How do you do that?"

"It's a mom's job to know. Spill it, kid!"

"Ella—" I said.

"Ella?" Mom repeated.

"She brought something over for me."

"Are you going to tell me, or do I need to guess?" Mom seemed frustrated.

"I'm just worried about your reaction."

"Honestly, after all we've been through the last month, R.J.—just tell me." Mom was definitely frustrated.

"What if I show you?"

"That's fine. Let's see it."

"Hold on. I left it in my room." I ran to my room, grabbed the cello case, and headed back toward the kitchen. I could feel my heart racing.

"A cello?"

"Yeah, it belongs to one of Ella's neighbors—some lady named Mrs. Monahan. Ella said I could use it to practice."

"I don't know, R.J. With the court case starting in a few days, I don't think we should have that in the house. It's just too dangerous. You've got to give it back."

"But how will I explain that? The details are already so complicated. She and her whole family know I'm the kid who played the cello for her sister's tribute concert. Fortunately, they believe my name really is R.J."

"Honey, I'm not sure having it here is a good idea. I'm hoping all this will be in the past very soon. We need to maintain our new status quo for the moment."

"Status quo? Wow, Mom! You're starting to sound like Marshal Stevens."

"Good. We need a little of that right now, especially since the court case is about to start. Dad's face will be plastered in the media across the United States. We can't take chances," said Mom.

"Status quo it is! For Dad!" I agreed.

"For Dad!" seconded Mom. "Now, let's get dinner started. Mallory should be home from practice in about an hour."

"Sounds like a plan. What are we having?"

"Stir-fried veggies and teriyaki chicken," Mom answered.

"Yum! Can't wait!"

CHAPTER TWENTY-SIX

THE KICKBALL TOURNAMENT

WEDNESDAY MORNING WAS FINALLY here. The sky was a brilliant shade of blue, not a cloud in sight. Mom dropped Mallory and me off at our schools and was heading back home to watch the court case. She had taken a personal day from work as she realized it would be too hard to focus knowing Dad was going to be live for all the world to see. She was trying to mask her concern by smiling and giving us a big wave as we said goodbye. I knew she was worried no matter how hard she tried to hide it. We were all worried.

Of course, she and Mallory were only

worried about Dad. Not that being worried for Dad wasn't huge, but I had something else to be worried about on top of that. Today was the fifth grade kickball tournament. As much as I wanted Dad home and our normal life back, something in me didn't want to miss the tournament. Somehow it had become important to me. I'm not sure exactly when it happened, but it did.

This synthetic life was messing me up. Nothing could ever replace my love for music and the cello, but the thought of winning the kickball tournament was pretty close to the feeling I had when I was on the stage. With the help of Ella, Blake, and Thomas, I managed to keep my improvement a secret from the rest of the class. Mr. Bailey had no idea that I could play without falling flat on my face. I have to give him credit. As much as we all knew he liked to win, he took time to make me feel comfortable.

"R.J., I know kickball may not be your thing, but I'm sure glad you're willing to give it a try. Just know I'm proud of you and the entire class no matter the outcome! Winning isn't everything. It's how we interact with one another that's more important."

"Thanks, Mr. Bailey. I appreciate your encouragement. I will try my best today."

"No worries. I can't ask for more than your best. And have fun!"

"Yes, sir!"

"You might want to tie your shoelaces before we head out to the field."

"Good catch, Mr. Bailey!" I knelt down to tie my laces before joining the class line. I could hear the other classes in the hall waiting to use the restroom. When I stood up, I saw Ella, Blake, and Thomas giving me a thumbs up.

"Hey, what's that about?" Andy asked getting in line behind me.

"Oh nothing. Just an inside joke." I smiled.

"Make sure you take your water bottles outside. The teachers have set up coolers for their classes. Our cooler is neon green—can't miss it! I put some snacks in it for each of you," Mr. Bailey announced as the students finished using the restrooms.

"What kind of snacks?" asked Charlie.

"Some of my favorites!"

"You mean Oreos, Chips Ahoy, cheese puffs, and donut holes from Dunkin' Donuts?"

"You know me too well, Charlie!" laughed Mr. Bailey. "I threw in some natural fruit snacks for good measure!"

"You're too funny, Mr. Bailey!" Charlie added.

"I aim to please. Now let's get going!"

After the quick bathroom break in the first and second grade hall, we headed out to the playground. I noticed blankets scattered around the sidelines and a few of the fourth grade classes making their way toward them. I didn't realize that we were going to have an audience. I hadn't thought about anyone watching besides the other fifth grade classes. This added element made me feel uneasy for some reason—something that I never experienced when playing the cello.

"Are you ready, R.J.?" Ella asked as she raced toward me.

"I thought I was." My voice sounded shaky.

"What's wrong? You've got this!" Ella seemed confused by my uncertainty.

"I didn't know the fourth grade was going to watch."

"Are you kidding me? Is that all you're worried about?" asked Ella.

"I haven't had time to process ..."

"Just imagine you're playing a concert.

You've played in front of thousands. How can you be rattled by a bunch of fourth graders?"

"Playing sports doesn't come natural to me. You know that!"

"I agree on one thing. Kickball didn't come natural to you, but you *learned*. You're really good now! I mean it. We're going to win, and Mr. Bailey will retain his title for the third consecutive year! Just remember the rhythm."

"Okay, I will. Thanks, Ella!"

"Don't let me down. After all, you're my Random Act of Kindness," Ella confessed.

"Huh?"

"You heard me. I added my post to Mr. Bailey's web page last night. You can read about it later. It's time for us to take our places. Here, give me your water bottle and I'll put it in the cooler."

"Thanks!"

Fifth grade classes were standing in one group and fourth grade classes in another as Mrs. Grant made her way to the microphone.

"Good morning, fifth grade competitors and fourth grade onlookers! We are so excited to announce the start of our Annual Fifth Grade Kickball Tournament. Before we begin, we will recite the Pledge of Allegiance." Voices recited the familiar words together:

> *I pledge allegiance to the Flag of the United States of America, and to the republic for which it stands, one nation under God, indivisible, with liberty and justice for all.*

Mrs. Grant paused then said, "Now, let's all recite our school pledge." Once again, voices joined hers, including mine.

> *As students of Fern Creek Elementary, we pledge to show kindness in all our words and actions in the hope that we will make a true difference in our school and the world beyond!*

"Now, let's play kickball!" Mrs. Grant called out.

The crowd roared with excitement when the fifth grade teachers, including Mr. Bailey, came running onto the field wearing cheerleader uniforms. He did a backward somersault midair, taking us all by surprise. A choreographed routine to "Eye of the Tiger" followed and received lots of cheers!

Sophie, Jennilee, and Andy had mentioned early on that this was an important event for fifth grade. I guess I didn't realize how big a deal it was. Once the teachers finished their routine, we were ready to begin. The kickball tournament was organized just like a real tournament. Two classes would play each other. The winning teams would then be paired up to play each other and the remaining two teams also played each other until the two teams that had the most wins would be paired up for the final game. The winner of the final game would be declared this year's champion.

Our class was paired against Mrs. Granger's class, and they were up first. We quickly took our positions on the field, and Thomas double-checked that we were ready before pitching the ball. The first kicker, wearing a serious expression, jumped in place as he waited for the ball to come barreling toward him. His foot hit the ball, propelling it toward third base. Spencer caught it before it hit the ground.

"You're out!" bellowed Assistant Principal Phillips. He was the official umpire for the game.

The next three players managed a base hit each, making the bases loaded. Next up was

Ty. His first attempt produced a foul ball. With the next kick, Ty's foot connected with the ball with a loud crack. It was heading straight for Jennilee who was ready for it. She caught the ball after one bounce, tagged the runner heading to second, then threw the ball toward home plate. Thomas caught it and tagged out the player heading home.

"Three outs! Switch!" shouted Mr. Phillips.

We were now up. Thomas called out the lineup, "Zoe, Andy, Ella, me, Sophie, Blake, Jennilee, Spencer, Emma, and R.J. If we get past the first ten then I'll call the next lineup!"

"Whoop! Whoop! You made the first ten, R.J.!" Ella shouted, shaking both hands in the air.

"Yeah, guess I did!" I shouted back feeling a bit uncertain.

"Let's go, Zoe!" Thomas howled as she made her way to home plate.

Looking toward the field, I noticed that Ty was pitching for his class. I'd seen him play during recess, and he was a pretty solid player. He pitched the ball and Zoe kicked a foul. On the second try, she managed to make it safely to second base. Andy did the same, but Zoe only made it to third base before the ball was back to home plate. Ella was awesome. She kicked a home run, allowing Zoe and Andy to make it home and putting us ahead at three points. Thomas kicked a fly ball, which was caught by Ty. He normally kicked them low and fast, but this time was different. Sophie made it to first base. Blake was up next. He kicked the ball, sending it directly down center field. Fortunately, the second baseman missed the ball as it zoomed past his feet, and Sophie made it safely to second before the ball was back to Ty.

Jennilee was up next. I sensed some nervous energy, which was unlike her. Maybe she wasn't exactly over Monday's conversation. That's the only way to explain her performance. She kicked three fouls before kicking the ball directly into Ty's arms. We now had two outs, but we were still winning. Spencer was up next. He kicked the ball directly down the first base line and made it safely to first base before he was tagged. Spencer was hands down the fastest runner in our class.

"You're safe!" Mr. Phillips bellowed.

Bases were loaded, and it was now Emma's turn. It was a huge relief knowing that I wasn't up next. I couldn't imagine the pressure she was feeling at that moment. But something was wrong. Instead of heading toward home plate, she was walking toward Mr. Bailey. Mr. Phillips called a timeout, and we all waited while Emma and Mr. Bailey talked. Mr. Bailey motioned for the nurse, who had Emma sit on the ground and drink orange juice.

"Emma's going to be fine. She just needs to sit out for a while. Move on to the next player," Mr. Bailey announced through the megaphone.

That was me! What? How? Why was this happening? I was number ten, not nine. Couldn't they put someone else in her place? My heart began beating harder. It was happening all over again!

"Let's go, R.J.! You're up!" Thomas shouted.

"You can do it, R.J.!" Blake cheered from second base.

"Remember, feel the rhythm!" Ella added from the fence.

I walked slowly toward home plate, taking deep breaths with each step. Images of Sunday's kickball game at the apartments flashed through my mind. I could see everyone cheering me on and having a great time. Looking up, I saw Ty staring directly at me. His eyes were fixed on me, and his nostrils flared a few times. I felt a surge of confidence. I took several steps back and waited for the ball to be pitched. Ty swooped the ball back before lunging it toward me. I followed the cadence of the ball with my body and at just the right time, I ran toward the ball, closed my eyes, and kicked it. The impact made a loud crack followed by an instantaneous silence. In that millisecond, I prepared myself for defeat but was thrown back into reality by the rousing cheers that came from the entire field.

"RUN, R.J.! Run!" shouted the entire class.

I started running toward first base and continued as the crowd kept chanting, "Run! Run! Run!" I arrived at second base, and the crowd kept going, so I did too. It continued past third and all the way to home plate. I had kicked a home run, the first ever for me! My whole class gathered around me, jumping up and down and screaming like we had won the World Series! We just scored four runs because of me! I couldn't believe it. The feelings I was now experiencing were exactly the same as those I felt when playing my music. How could this be? I am a musician, not an athlete. But with the help of Ella, Blake, and Thomas, I was able to experience success where I once felt dread.

"Way to go, R.J! That was AWE-some!" a voice called out from the field. It was Ty. He was giving me a thumbs up and smiling. I couldn't believe what I was seeing. At that moment, I didn't care about the home run. Knowing that my Random Act of Kindness truly made a difference in someone's life trumped the excitement of a homerun. No matter the outcome of the tournament, I felt like a winner!

Our class continued its winning streak throughout the morning, and about an hour after lunch, we found ourselves playing against Mrs. Hamilton's class for the championship. The sun's relentless heat was getting the best of us. It was turning into the warmest day of the season with no sign of relief. The game was long and tense, as both classes vied for the win. We remained tied for almost an hour, and it seemed that an end was nowhere in sight. We were up. Zoe and Andy had managed to make it safely to second and third base, respectively. Unfortunately, we also had two outs and one more out would bring on at least one more round of play. Ella took a deep breath as she walked toward home plate. She looked tired but determined.

"Go, Ella! You've got this!" I shouted from the fence. Others followed suit. She turned and smiled at me before taking a few steps backward. Watching the ball roll toward her, I could feel the rhythm in my body. Her foot hit the ball straight on, and it went torpedoing down right field between first and second base. Its force caused it to slip right out of the hands of the outfield player, seemingly caught off guard by its appearance. Ella had kicked a winner, bringing in enough runs to bring us ahead by two points. We had won the tournament! Instantly, Mr. Bailey was doing a celebratory dance on the sidelines, which was beyond ridiculous, but we all joined in without hesitation. The fourth graders cheered us on, and before Mr. Phillips made his way to the mic, the whole crowd had joined us in the absurd dance ritual. It looked like a flash mob, and I loved every minute. At that moment, the events of the last month were not at the forefront of my mind. I was not feeling the weight of the unknown on my shoulders. I felt free.

Unfortunately, reality is a killjoy. The look on Mom's face when I opened the car door in the car ride line was all it took.

CHAPTER TWENTY-SEVEN

IT'S NOT LOOKING GOOD

MOM'S FACE APPEARED TEAR-STAINED, and I hesitated to say anything about my day in fear that it would seem insensitive. I sat quietly thumbing through the final chapters of a book in my backpack. When I found myself reading the same paragraph three times, I closed the book and tossed it back into my backpack. Within minutes, Mom pulled into our parking space. We both got out of the car without a word between us, but Mom smiled at me as we walked up the stairs. The silence was deafening. I put my backpack down and ran into the bathroom to wash up from the day.

A phone rang, and I heard Mom answer it after the second ring. It wasn't her regular ring tone, so I figured it was the special phone. Something was definitely wrong, and this phone call made it certain. I couldn't make out what Mom was saying. I walked into the kitchen, grabbed a snack, and sat at the counter. From outside, I could hear Mallory talking to a neighbor. She was home earlier than usual.

"You're home early," I declared as Mallory walked through the door.

"Yeah, I didn't stay for practice today. Hey, why isn't the TV on? I thought Mom would be watching the trial."

"I think something is wrong," I said quietly.

"Did Mom say anything?"

"No."

"So, why do you think something is wrong?"

"She hasn't said a single word since I got into the car at school. And now she's on the special phone, so—"

"That doesn't mean anything. This should be an open and shut case. Dad should be ready to come home soon."

"I don't know, Mal. I'm starting to think that we will be stuck with this life forever."

"What's gotten into you, R.J.? Stop being negative." Mallory put down her gear and grabbed a banana from the fruit bowl.

"I'm not being negative! Something is wrong. Mom's face was—"

"He's right, Mallory," interrupted Mom.

"What's wrong?" Mallory asked, putting down the banana.

"I just got off the phone with Marshal Stevens. He has given me some insight into what is happening in the trial."

"Mom, tell us already! I can't stand not knowing," Mallory pleaded.

"The court proceedings started around nine this morning. The major networks began televising around ten, just as the lawyers were making their opening statements. The prosecuting attorney seemed pretty solid. But then the lawyers for the defense spoke." Mom sighed before continuing, "They are trying to put the blame for the negligence on a bio-chemist—"

"You mean Dad?" Mallory interrupted.

"Unfortunately, yes," Mom confirmed.

"What? Dad had nothing to do with the bad stuff! Why are they doing this to him—to us? And who is the prosecutor?" I asked on the verge of tears.

"Honey, it's all part of their strategy. They are trying to discredit the main witness with the jury. If they can paint a negative picture of Dad, then maybe his testimony will be dismissed," Mom explained.

"What did Marshal Stevens say?" Mallory asked, now trying to comfort me.

"Well, he said that I shouldn't worry. The prosecutor, the lawyer presenting the case against the corrupt company officers, feels strongly that the transcript from the conversations between Dad and the investors—"

"When Dad was wearing the wire?" I asked, interrupting Mom.

"Yes. He feels that there is enough evidence in those conversations to put the officers away in jail for a long time—and take action against the corrupt foreign investors as well. We just need to be patient. The defense attorneys don't have a leg to stand on, so they are going to do everything possible to discredit Dad. Marshal Stevens reminded me to be extremely careful not to give away our identities. We are in the most danger during the trial. These investors will try anything to shut Dad up to protect themselves. We've got to act as normal as possible in our new identities. I know I failed miserably this afternoon. Marshal Stevens' phone call was my wake-up call. I need to be strong for all of us."

"Mom, you are always strong! I don't know anyone who could handle this better than you," Mallory said, giving Mom a big hug.

"Thanks, honey! But you two have been amazing. I couldn't ask for two more brilliant, talented, and resilient children. Dad and I are truly blessed. When this is over, we're all going to need a long vacation," Mom added, hugging us both.

"So, how long did Marshal Stevens say it would take?" I asked, hoping for a reasonable time.

"There's no way of knowing, honey. It's going to depend on the lawyers and the jury. Once the lawyers have pleaded their case, the jury goes behind closed doors to discuss the evidence and reach a consensus," explained Mom.

"A consensus?" I asked.

"A unified agreement," Mallory explained.

"What if some of them don't agree? Does that mean the lawyers have to start all over again?" I asked, hoping the answer would be what I wanted to hear.

"No, the attorneys don't need to do

anything. The jurors have to keep deliberating—considering the evidence—until they reach an agreement or verdict," Mom answered.

"We just discussed this in my American Government class," Mallory said, pulling out the notes from her backpack. "I find the judicial system so interesting. Maybe I'll be a lawyer."

"I could see you as a lawyer," Mom agreed.

"Yeah, she's always talking her way out of things!" I added, giving Mallory an elbow in the ribs.

"Like you don't ..."

"All right, you two—give it a rest. You know, with all that's happened I completely forgot to ask you about the kickball tournament."

"Yeah, how did it go?" Mallory inquired, forgetting about my last comment.

"I think it went okay."

"Okay? What does that mean?" inquired Mallory.

"We kind of ..."

"You're killing me, R.J.! Spill it!" Mallory pleaded.

"Won!" I said, beaming ear to ear.

"That's fantastic, honey!" Mom's smile was back.

"Did you manage to make it on base?" Mallory asked.

"Did I manage to make it on base? Are you kidding me? I kicked a grand slam on my first try!" I couldn't help the dramatics. This was huge for me.

"Well, I'll be—" Mallory started.

"A monkey's uncle!" I quipped.

"I'll show you a monkey's uncle!" Mallory grabbed me and began to tickle me. She knew my tickle spot, and as much as I fought it, I couldn't hold back the laughter.

CHAPTER TWENTY-EIGHT

SIXTH GRADE BOOT CAMP

THE NEXT FEW DAYS were a mixed bag of emotions, but I managed to keep them in check for Dad's sake and our safety. Mr. Bailey dusted off the Kickball Tournament trophy and placed it at the front of our classroom on a pedestal he found in the storage room. He was completely stoked with our accomplishment, and we felt the benefit—no homework assignments were written on the board! Instead, Mr. Bailey grabbed a large rolled banner and unfurled it across the space directly in front of the board. We thought it was going to say congrats or something along those lines. But that was far from the direction Mr. Bailey had in mind. As the banner spread across the floor, we read the words in unison.

"Welcome to Sixth Grade Boot Camp!"

"Huh? What's Sixth Grade Boot Camp, Mr. Bailey?" Thomas asked.

"Yeah, Mr. Bailey. We're confused. What does Sixth Grade Boot Camp have to do with our win?" Jennilee asked.

Mr. Bailey smiled and said, "Absolutely nothing."

"Are we getting a visit from the middle school?" Thomas, who was usually pretty level-headed, appeared unraveled.

"No, not exactly. We're going to begin a review for the end-of-year exams, which will directly affect your sixth-grade year," responded Mr. Bailey.

Zoe, who was now sitting up on her knees asked, "Wait, how do our scores affect sixth grade?"

"Before I answer, Miss Milton and everyone, please sit properly in your chairs."

"Oh, sorry, Mr. Bailey!"

"Well … your scores will determine the type of classes you can choose from—remedial, regular, or advanced. From what I can tell, most of you will have a mix of regular and advanced classes. You have all worked hard and learned so much this year. We're going to spend the next few weeks reviewing and sharpening our skillsets. Yes, Sophie."

"Mr. Bailey, you've just made me so nervous! What if I completely bomb the tests?"

"The end-of-year assessments are no harder than any of the other tests you have tackled all year. They just take a little longer and have a scarier name. There's no need to worry; you've all scored well in prior elementary grades, so nothing should be a surprise." Mr. Bailey smiled, but I could tell that some of the students didn't find his comments reassuring.

"But everyone has a bad day every once in a while. What if that happens on the day of one of the tests?" Zoe's voice quivered as she spoke.

"Honestly, I don't think any of you need to worry. Your confidence should be through the roof! Come on, guys! It's really going to be fine!"

Sitting there listening to everyone, I knew I had something valuable to say, something that would make everyone feel better. My hand went up.

Mr. Bailey said, "Yes, Mr. Baker."

"As many of you know, I had a fear of sports when I entered this room back in April. Thanks to a few students—I mean friends—in this class, I have learned to conquer my fears and turn a weakness into a strength. Mr. Bailey is just like those friends. He has worked with our class and has helped bring out the best in each of us. I'm sure he's turned many weaknesses into strengths. All we need to do is our personal best. We've got this. I just know it!"

"R.J., I couldn't have explained it any better!" Mr. Bailey was beaming, and I could see smiles appearing on the faces of my classmates.

Suddenly, a few students began to chant, "We've got this! We've got this!"

The whole class joined in, including Mr. Bailey. It continued until Mrs. Grant entered the room.

"Is everything okay, Mr. Bailey?" Mrs. Grant asked.

"Absolutely, Mrs. Grant! Did you need me?"

"I just came to congratulate your students on a splendid victory yesterday. I wish I could have been there for the whole event. Mr. Phillips shared the wonderful display of sportsmanship demonstrated by all students, and the whole school is still buzzing about Mr. Baker's display of athleticism. I hear it was quite impressive! The trophy seems destined to remain in your room, Mr. Bailey!"

"It sure seems that way, Mrs. Grant! Thank you for taking the time to come by our room this morning. We know how busy this time of year is for you!" Mr. Bailey looked at us, and we knew what he wanted.

"Thank you, Mrs. Grant!" the class exclaimed in unison.

"You're all very welcome! Have a wonderful day!"

Mrs. Grant gave us two thumbs up and made her way out the door. When we thought she was far enough down the hall, we took up a new chant, using the quietest whisper voices we could muster, "We can do it! We can do it! We can do it!"

The chanting subsided with a wave of Mr. Bailey's hand. He explained the schedule and how each day would look. I could tell he had spent time thinking about this plan. It was pretty intense with a mix of awesome. He knew exactly how to balance work with fun. That's what made him such a great teacher.

CHAPTER TWENTY-NINE

EVERYTHING IS BETTER WITH CHOCOLATE CHIP PANCAKES

ON SATURDAY MORNING, MALLORY spent nearly thirty minutes sharing insights from her classmates about the televised trial. It was interesting to hear the range of thoughts, although I was a little weirded out when so many girls thought the witness for the prosecuting attorney was a "hottie." That hottie was my dad! I don't think I'll ever understand teenage girls. Why would they think a man old enough to be their dad is a hottie? It was weird. Mallory seemed to think it was funny, and Mom appeared to take it as a compliment.

I was outnumbered, so I decided to change the subject.

"Today is the day I was supposed to play at Carnegie Hall," I announced bringing the last conversation to a halt. Mom and Mallory looked at each other, hoping to find the right words.

"I know, honey." Mom's voice seemed strained. "There will be other invites."

"But what if they can't forgive the fact that we fell off the face of the earth. No communication with anyone from our real life!" I could feel my face begin to turn red.

"They'll understand, R.J., especially if the U.S. Marshals Service explains the situation," Mallory added, trying to help calm me down.

"You don't have a second chance for a first impression, isn't that what Dad always says?"

"But this is different!" objected Mallory.

"She's right, R.J. This will be over soon, and things will be back to normal. You'll see! What if I make some chocolate chip pancakes to help brighten the day?"

"Can you add extra chocolate chips?

"I think that's possible." Mom smiled at the two of us as she began gathering the ingredients.

"I'll help!" announced Mallory.

"You know I never refuse help. Grab the eggs from the fridge, please."

Mom makes some of the best chocolate chip pancakes around. Dad would often try to sneak the first few warm off the skillet, but not today. Watching the plate fill up as Mom and Mallory worked together, I felt such a love for my family. Not every kid is blessed with great parents, and those of us who are often don't realize it. At least not until we're older. This synthetic life is feeling more like a blessing rather than a curse. I'm still a musician, but now I can play kickball.

Who would have guessed that this would ever happen? Wait until Uncle Seth sees me in action. For once in his life, he'll be speechless. I'll have to share my new skills with him. I'm sure he'll be all in. I hope the news he was going to share with us is about him getting married. Wait, what if he's already married? He always said I would be his best man. Nah, Uncle Seth would wait for us! My thoughts were interrupted by a knock at the door. Swallowing the last bite of pancake, I wiped my mouth, and headed for the door.

"Hey, Ella! I wasn't expecting you this

early. Do you want some chocolate chip pancakes? Mom just made them."

"No, I'm good. My family is waiting for me in the parking lot. We're going to visit my grandparents for the weekend. I completely forgot to tell you yesterday."

"No problem. That's great, but you could have called instead of coming by."

"I know. I just needed to tell you something important," she said.

"Oh, okay. What is it?" I asked.

"We know," she answered.

"You know?"

"We saw part of the trial," she responded.

"Oh, um …"

"Don't worry. We get it."

"All of you?" I asked.

"Yes."

"It's—" I started to say.

"We know," she interjected.

"I can't—"

"Like I said, we get it. No need to worry. Have a great weekend. I'll see you Monday at school. Bye!" she said as she turned and ran down the stairs.

"Bye!"

"Who was at the door?" Mom asked.

"Ella."

"Where did she go?"

"She had to leave. She and her family are driving to her grandparents' farm for the weekend."

"Oh, so why did she stop by?"

"Mom, they know."

"Oh ..." Mom said.

"She said they get it and not to worry."

"I see. Let's hope they really do understand and will keep the secret." Mom seemed a little concerned.

"Yep."

We stood there watching Ella and her family pull out of the parking lot and drive off. A few months from eleven years old and already I knew that sometimes life could be more complex than most kids ever fathomed. It's a million little things that somehow come together to create moments. Some moments will be forgotten quickly while others will stay with us for life. These moments don't stop, and they don't care if we're living with an authentic or a synthetic identity. Life happens. It's that simple.

CHAPTER THIRTY

A CHANGE OF HEART

ELLA KEPT TRUE TO her word. During the next two weeks, she never brought up the conversation or even hinted about our secret. Her friendship meant so much, and I was glad she never gave up on me. Mr. Bailey kept us extremely busy reviewing everything that could possibly show up on the end-of-grade assessments. We were thoroughly prepared and confident. Until I met Mr. Bailey, I thought no teachers could compare to my teachers at The Briarcliffe School for the Performing Arts.

Mr. Bailey is a force to be reckoned. He is so caring with his students and has personally challenged me academically to achieve even more. He is the master at helping students make connections in learning, and I think I'm actually smarter now than I was six weeks ago. Imagine if I had spent this entire year in his class. If only he knew how much he has helped me conquer my fears.

That quote above his door no longer seemed absurd. "The only thing we have to fear is fear itself." Sure, I realize that it was first quoted by Franklin D. Roosevelt during his first Inaugural Address. Our country was in the Great Depression, and he had to change mindsets. I guess that's the same task Mr. Bailey faces when a new group of students enters his classroom each year. We walk in carrying our strengths like medals pinned on our shirts, but we keep our weaknesses and fears hidden.

Mr. Bailey unearths our fears not so we can be embarrassed but rather to help us conqueror them. When I'm finally able to be Preston Alexander Davis again, I know I will be all the better because of what I have learned as R.J. Baker. I hope I have the opportunity to tell Mr. Bailey just how much Preston has grown as an individual. Maybe someday soon.

CHAPTER THIRTY-ONE

SHARK TANK

TWO WEEKS FLEW BY so quickly, especially with all that was transpiring in our lives. The end-of-grade assessments were happening all week long, and the jury was preparing to head into deliberations as the lawyers completed closing arguments. It seemed to be clear, at least to us, that the "investors" and the company were guilty, but Mom said one can never really tell what a jury will do. The lawyers for the defense were sharks surrounding the witnesses trying to chew them up and discount their testimony. They were masters at spinning the truth and intimidating the witnesses, something adults kept saying in sidebar conversations throughout town.

Mom was confident Dad would come out of all this unscathed, and our lives would go back to the familiar. Mallory and I were hoping she was right, but until we heard the verdict, we were afraid to stop holding our breath.

Sure, some things about this synthetic life were not as bad as we had initially anticipated. Mallory's team won the regional soccer championship thanks to her mad passing skills. I think this life-altering change has made her faster and more precise. She was amazing before, but now I think she has stepped up to be exceptional.

As for me, I know my life has been changed for the better. In fact, if I could play the cello again, I almost wouldn't mind living life as R.J. Okay, maybe I'd grow my hair out again and ditch the contacts, but I could live with the rest pretty easily. Losing the fear of playing sports is probably my most significant accomplishment. The students at Briarcliffe would flip out if they could see me in action. Heck, I'm still flipping out. On second thought, facing my bully was probably my biggest success. The possibility that I might have actually helped Ty is an unexpected but welcome bonus.

"Mallory! R.J.! Come see this! Hurry!" Mom called out from the living room.

I jumped off my bed and ran to the living room, almost colliding with Mallory as she was vying for the same spot on the couch. Mom was watching the trial, and the jury was about to enter the courtroom to read their verdict.

"What are they saying?" Mallory asked.

"Nothing yet, honey," answered Mom.

"It looks like they're coming in now!" I added from my spot on the floor directly in front of the screen.

"R.J., move over so we can see! Now!" protested Mallory.

"Okay, Okay!" I moved over and grabbed the remote to turn up the volume.

The camera zoomed in on the judge as he waited for the jury to take their seats. He appeared calm, but it was apparent that the long days had worn him out. As the last juror took her place, the jury foreman handed the bailiff some papers. The bailiff walked over to the judge and handed him the documents. The judge put on his glasses and carefully reviewed the pages. This process seemed to last forever, and we were anxious to hear the verdict. Finally, the judge handed the papers back to the bailiff and addressed the foreman.

"Mister Foreman, how do you find the defendants?"

The foreman, a middle-aged man with a receding hairline, stood up and addressed the judge. "We, the jury, upon our oaths, unanimously find the defendant, Bio-Logics Pharmaceuticals Holding Company, guilty of extortion as charged in Count 1 of the indictment. We, the jury, upon our oaths, unanimously find the defendant, Bio-Logics Pharmaceutical Holding Company, guilty of embezzlement as charged in count 2 of the indictment. We, the jury, upon our oaths, unanimously find the defendant, Bio-Logics Pharmaceutical Holding Company, guilty of tampering with consumer products as charged in count 3 of the indictment."

Mom stood up, tears now streaming down her face. She didn't say a word, but we knew something had broken open inside her. For the first time since this whole ordeal began, she was completely unhinged. Mom had been our rock, steady and unwavering, never complaining about walking away from a job she adored. Seeing her now in this state, I realized that she had been stable for us. I never once considered how she felt going through this process. How could I have been so selfish? Surely I still had a lot to learn about life.

"Does this mean Dad is coming home? Or are we going home to Dad?" Mallory asked, hoping to get an answer from Mom in her current state.

"I'm not sure which one, Mila—but Dad will be with us soon!"

"Does that mean we can go back to our real identities?" Mila asked, hugging Mom.

"Yes! Marshal Stevens said if the verdict came in their favor, we could return to our former lives. But we'll probably need to wait until we hear from them."

"Do you hear that, Preston?" Mila asked, beaming from ear to ear.

"Yes, Mila!" I said emphatically. It felt so good to hear and use our real names again.

The three of us had a hug-fest until we were interrupted by the phone ringing. It was Marshal Stevens. Mom seemed to be on the phone for an eternity as Mila and I waited anxiously for the details. Mom's dialogue was useless. It was a mix of "I understand" and

"Okay" with an occasional "I see." Finally, she ended the call with, "That sounds like the best plan. Thank you again, Marshal Stevens!"

"So, what did he say?" I asked.

The judge continued speaking, so my answer had to wait. "The sentencing for the defendants, the officers of the Bio-Logics Pharmaceutical Holding Company, will be held one week from today at 10:00 a.m. Officers, please take the defendants away." The cameraman zoomed in on the defendants as the officers headed toward them.

"So, what did Marshal Stevens say?" I asked again.

"Dad will be arriving in Portland late Thursday afternoon, and we can resume our identities once he gets here. Since the school year is about over, Marshal Stevens thought we should wait a few more weeks before packing up and heading home. This will give Dad some time to see where we've been living and get him away from all the publicity related to the case."

"You mean the paparazzi?" asked Mila.

"Dad's a celebrity? That's awesome!" I couldn't help myself.

Mom smiled then added, "More like a

SHARK TANK • 197

hero. I guess in some eyes Dad can be considered a celebrity."

"Wow, Dad is a bona fide hero!" Mila beamed with pride. "Wait till my friends hear this!"

"I'm sure they already know about it back home." I didn't mean to burst her bubble, but all of our friends would have recognized Dad on the television.

"Not my friends back home, silly, my new friends here!"

"Oh, yeah, that's right! Everyone here thinks we're the Bakers, well except for Ella and her family. Cool. I can't wait to tell mine either!"

Mom said, "Dad has been offered a job with another pharmaceutical lab and will start once we get back home. The U.S. Marshals Service is covering our expenses for the next few months until everything settles down."

"That's awesome, Mom!" Mila shouted, jumping around the room like she had just won the lottery. "That means I can lead my team in the State Championship games, and Dad can be here to cheer us on!"

It was a good day in the Davis, also known as Baker, apartment. A really good day!

CHAPTER THIRTY-TWO

HOLDING BACK

GLANCING AT THE CLOCK on the class-room wall, I couldn't believe only a minute had passed since my last check. We were in the middle of our final assessment, and I was having a hard time keeping my mind focused on math knowing that Dad was on his way. Other than the occasional business trip, which generally lasted no more than three days, our family had never been separated.

Dad was such an important part of the family. He wasn't the typical science geek; Dad was cool. He danced with Mom whenever their favorite songs played on the radio—even in

public! Dad kept a notebook, a sort of journal.
I peeked inside it once and read an assortment
of scribbled notes and doodles. He wrote things
like, "Mila was a beast on the field today, and
I couldn't be prouder." "Preston's performance
of Bach's Cello Suite No. 1, The Prelude was
mesmerizing." and "Looking at my wife's face
as the early light of morning highlights her natural beauty, I am smitten all over again!" In
Mom's words, "Dad is a keeper," and I couldn't
wait to give him the biggest hug and tell him all
about the last few months, especially the kickball tournament. He'll probably come up with
some silly new moves or a quirky saying.

I glanced at the clock again. It was not
moving any faster. I decided to focus my attention on the math in front of me. The assessment
was actually quite easy, and once I made it a
point to focus, I was finished in no time at all.
As Mr. Bailey collected the last assessment
booklets, I saw Mrs. Grant peering through
window in our classroom door. She waited for
Mr. Bailey to place the answer sheets and booklets in the testing container before entering our
room.

"Hello, Mr. Bailey," Mrs. Grant said as
she did a quick scan of the room.

"Hello, Mrs. Grant. Is there a problem?" Mr. Bailey asked, wondering why she had come.

"No, Mr. Bailey, on the contrary. I have some special guests who are quite eager to see one of your students. They've been sharing some extraordinary details with me during the last hour. Why don't you drop off your assessments while I stay with your class? The guests are waiting in the office. If you don't mind, please escort them to your room as you make your way back."

"Sure, Mrs. Grant. You've piqued my curiosity, and I can't wait to meet these guests!" Mr. Bailey quickly made his way out of the room with the testing container in hand.

Mrs. Grant used her walkie-talkie to call the front office.

"Office, pick up."

"Yes, Mrs. Grant," responded the receptionist.

"Mr. Bailey is on his way. Please have the guests walk back with him to his classroom."

"Yes, will do. Anything else?" the receptionist asked.

Yes, please make an announcement that all assessments have been completed for the year!"

"I'll get right on it!"

Everyone in class began wondering who the special guests were coming to see. Various students started asking Mrs. Grant for some hints, but she didn't budge. "You'll soon find out," was her only response.

I tracked Mr. Bailey's route in my mind to help the time move quicker. I even paused so he could take a bathroom break. As I imagined him climbing back up the stairs, the office made the announcement over the loudspeaker that all assessments had been completed for this year. As our class cheered, I was more excited than anyone else but for a different reason. It had to be Dad coming with Mr. Bailey, and I could hardly wait for them to arrive. Suddenly, the door opened, and Mr. Bailey entered the room alone. Where was Dad?

"Class, I would like to introduce Mr. and Mrs. Davis, Preston's parents," Mr. Bailey announced, extending his hand toward the door.

Mom and Dad entered the classroom, and all I wanted to do was run to them and jump into Dad's arms, just like I used to do when I was little. It took everything in me to stay seated and wait until my emotions stabilized so

I wouldn't make a total fool of myself. Confusion settled on the classroom.

"Hey, isn't he the guy from that court case?" Andy inquired, pointing to the man now standing beside Mr. Bailey.

"Yeah, that is the same man who testified in that court case last week," Angelica added.

"Mr. Bailey, who in the world is Preston?" Jennilee called out, trying to be heard among the clamoring voices.

"Yeah, there isn't a Preston in this room!" Thomas said.

"Oh, I beg to differ, Thomas," Mr. Bailey retorted.

"Then where is he?" questioned Thomas.

"I'm right here," I announced, standing up. The class was instantly silenced.

"Huh? What are you talking about, R.J.? Is this a joke?" Jennilee asked me.

"No, not at all. My name isn't R.J. Baker. It's Preston Alexander Davis, and these are my parents." I still wanted to run and hug Dad, but I knew I would have to wait.

"Mrs. Grant, would you like to explain?" Mr. Bailey asked, looking for support.

"Absolutely, Mr. Bailey," she replied, eager to share the information. For the next thirty minutes, Mrs. Grant, along with my parents, explained the events that had catapulted my family into this synthetic life.

The students listened in awe to every detail, occasionally looking back at me to see my response. With each detail spoken, I could literally feel my real identity return until I was no longer R.J. It was finally over, and I almost couldn't believe it.

CHAPTER THIRTY-THREE

EARTH TO PRESTON

LAYERS OF FEAR AND anxiety continued to peel away as the day worked its way into the evening. Eating dinner around the table once again as a family made me feel complete. In the recesses of my mind, I knew that this present reality was, in many ways, altered from what we once knew and somehow, I didn't mind. Listening to Dad's conversation with Mila about high school antics and Mom's hilarious stories about her retail job was soothing—the more they soaked in, the more I felt like a Davis. I was so caught up in the moment I didn't hear Dad calling my name.

"Preston. Preston. Earth to Preston. Hello!" Dad's voice grew a bit louder with each word until I finally was awakened from my trance.

"Oh, sorry Dad. I was—"

"Daydreaming?" Mila interrupted, grabbing another spoonful of Mom's garlic mashed potatoes.

"He's been through a tough few months, honey. Don't be so hard on him," Dad said, waiting for Mila to return the spoon so he could get his own second helping.

"Like we haven't?" Mila retorted.

"We all have, but Preston had to change his look completely and then face some challenges for the first time," added Mom coming to my rescue.

"I know. You're right. That doesn't mean that it hasn't been hard on the rest of us. I had to give up my cell phone, social media, and all my friends." Then turning to me she continued, "Dude, you have to admit that this whole experience has made you stronger. In my eyes, you're more like a real kid—still talented beyond words, but now I can play kickball with you!"

"Kickball?" Dad put down his fork.

"Okay, spill the beans."

I shared every detail over Mom's most famous dessert—red velvet cake with buttercream frosting. Dad had two large pieces, and Mom didn't say a word about his splurge. She would typically tap the table like she was sending a Morse code message whenever Dad went for seconds on dessert. This time, she didn't even tap once. Looking at her smile as I poured out my story to Dad, I saw my mom again, even through the frumpy hairstyle—which had begun to grow out—and the horn-rimmed glasses. Soon, we would all be back in our home in Chicago and finally find out if Uncle Seth was engaged. What's a little more suspense in the big scheme of things? Being best man at Uncle Seth's wedding would be a piece of cake after all we've endured.

CHAPTER THIRTY-FOUR

ELLA'S BIG SURPRISE

THE LAST DAY OF school was quickly approaching, and the classroom was beginning to look bare as Mr. Bailey took down our work and returned projects. I couldn't believe how much work I had completed in just two months of school. Since Mr. Bailey made learning so interesting and hands-on, each task seemed more like an exploration rather than work. I noticed that Ella wasn't in school today though I had seen her sister as I headed toward the fifth grade hall. Maybe Ella was sick. Summer colds are the worst! Mr. Bailey was having us sort novels when Ella walked in the classroom with

Mrs. Grant. They both seemed eager to share some news with the class. Mr. Bailey walked over to them and spent a few minutes chatting before announcing, "Boys and girls, please stop what you're doing for a few minutes and return to your seats. Mrs. Grant and Ella have some exciting news."

"Actually, Ella has some exciting news to share," corrected Mrs. Grant.

"Yes, I do," Ella chimed in, pausing to take a deep breath. "My parents and I have known about R.J.'s, I mean Preston's, amazing talent since he first entered our school. It was actually my sister Natalia who recognized him first. Although we couldn't remember at the time that his name was Preston Davis, we knew he was the brilliant musician who played for my older sister's tribute concert. I promised to keep his talent a secret. Then when we saw Mr. Davis on television, we knew he was R.J.—I mean Preston's dad because we had seen him at the concert for my sister. And besides *Preston* looks a lot like his dad!

We started doing some research. A few weeks ago, Preston was supposed to be a guest musician at Carnegie Hall. For those of you who might not know, this is a really great honor and a big deal. Of course, he couldn't make it because of the court case and all the witness protection stuff. So, my dad made some calls last week after Mr. and Mrs. Davis visited our class, and with the help of a very obliging U.S. Marshal, my dad was able to pull some strings."

"Tell us already!" Andy called out.

"Andy, hush!" Sophie reprimanded him.

"Sorry, I didn't mean for this to be so dramatic, but this is pretty big," Ella apologized before continuing. "In less than three hours, the entire New York Symphony Orchestra will be flying in for a special concert tomorrow night at the Portland Theater featuring our very own Preston Davis on the cello! And we're all invited!"

"Wow, our whole class is invited to the Portland Theater! That's so cool!" exclaimed Jennilee.

Mrs. Grant corrected, "No, not just your class, Jennilee—the whole school!"

"Are you kidding, Mrs. Grant?" asked Thomas.

"No, she's not kidding!" Ella chimed in as she looked at me.

"But I don't have my cello here. Well, I guess I can use Mrs. Monahan's cello. It's still in my closet," I was trying to keep my excitement in check, but secretly I wished I had my own cello.

"I don't think you need to worry about that," Ella added, grinning from ear-to-ear.

"What do you mean?" I asked.

"Oh, you'll see soon enough," she answered with a wink.

"Boys and girls, a few of the office staff, along with a room full of volunteers are in the process of contacting all Fern Creek Elementary parents with the details. I, for one, cannot wait to hear Preston play the cello! We hope all of you can be there!" Mrs. Grant's voice was even more animated than usual.

"My first symphony musical," Andy said, patting me on the back.

"He means symphony concert," corrected Sophie.

"He knows what I mean," rebutted Andy.

"Whatever!" Sophie said, then turned to ask Ella what she should wear.

As I stood there absorbing every detail of Ella's announcement, I realized that these students had become a vital part of my fifth grade experience. They, without any choice, had unknowingly joined me on my journey. They accepted and supported me as a classmate and friend. Now, watching their reaction to Ella's announcement, I knew they were along for the duration, and that was a pretty amazing feeling. It was a big deal. A *really* big deal.

BACH CELLO SUITE NO. 1 IN G MAJOR

WITH THE SOUND CHECK complete, the director raised his baton and commenced the rehearsal. The rhythm came alive in me, and I closed my eyes and began to play. The synchronous sound of each instrument filled the stage and echoed through the hall as if beckoning listeners. I had missed this so much, yet in a mere few seconds, it was as if I had never lost a day. The music was still as alive in me as it was before, but somehow my experiences over the last few months brought a new layer of emotion to the sound my bow produced. As the piece came to a dramatic end, I felt a stream of tears run down my cheek. The conductor didn't say a word. His head tilted ever so slightly in the direction of the score. Then he stood, turned toward me, and began to applaud. The others followed suit and applause filled the entire room. I was speechless. Was it possible that my experiences away from my cello only brought me closer to its true potential?

"Bravo! Bravo, Preston!" lauded the conductor.

Not knowing exactly what to do, I stood up and began thanking them. I had experienced applause many times, but this was different. This praise came from my musical peers, and it meant more to me than I could say.

As this was happening, I could hear some intermittent movement and chatter coming from the wings. The conductor signaled the stage manager, and he spoke into his headset. Within seconds, Ella, Mr. Bailey, Mrs. Grant, and Marshal Stevens walked onto the stage carrying a cello case. They stopped beside me and waited for direction. The conductor gave a single nod, and Ella stepped forward.

"Preston, on behalf of our school, the New York Symphony Orchestra, and the U.S.

Marshals Service, we would like to present you with a Man Claw, no I mean a Man Clay ... okay, it's a really expensive, handmade cello from Italy." Ella managed to get it all out even though she was as nervous as a fly caught in a spider's web.

"A Man Claudiu cello? Are you for real?" I asked, feeling like I was in a dream that was about to end at any second.

"Yes, and so that's how you say it!" Ella laughed at herself, then gave me a quick hug.

"Preston, your playing was breathtaking," Mrs. Grant said as she and Mr. Bailey stepped aside so that Marshal Stevens could hand me the case.

"Here you go, young man! That's some talent you have. The U.S. Marshals Service wishes you and your family the best. Thanks for handling the last few months so well. I'm so glad I can be here tonight. I even brought my wife and kids to hear you play. They are so excited, especially my son, Daniel, who has been taking violin lessons since he was five." For the first time, Marshal Stevens seemed like a regular guy, not so official.

"Marshal Stevens, Mrs. Grant, Mr. Bailey, Ella, and members of the New York Symphony

Orchestra, thank you for this unbelievable surprise. I saw one of these on display at Lincoln Center a few years ago and hoped that I could someday play one during a concert. Thank you for the opportunity to play one tonight. I promise to handle it gently." I was hoping Dad could video the performance. I knew I would remember this experience for the rest of my life.

"Preston, don't you get it? It's not on *loan*, it's yours, silly! You don't have to give it back!" Ella gave me a wide grin, and the whole stage began laughing.

"Are you kidding? Really? Wow! This is a-mazing!" Clearly, I was not coming up with the right words to express my gratitude.

"Just keep playing music and kickball!" Mr. Bailey said, coming to my rescue.

After a giving me some time to become acquainted with my new cello, the conductor had us run through a few more pieces until we retreated to the green room to freshen up before the concert.

That night there was not an empty seat in the house. The theater bustled with excitement as the house lights dimmed and the curtain rose. Walking onto the stage, I was greeted by a massive round of applause, and I could feel my cheeks burn from the overwhelming gratitude that welled up inside me. I sat, rested my hand on the neck of my cello, raised my bow, and waited for the conductor to begin.

The evening's selections were a mix of classical pieces and popular animated movie scores. I knew the conductor had chosen wisely as there was a little something for everyone. Before the last note faded, the entire audience was on its feet applauding and cheering. I could hear that cheer in my thoughts for months to follow, and the look on Dad's face was priceless. The journey was nearly over, and this was a last stop before reaching our final destination— home. I couldn't have imagined a better place than right here, right now.

EARLY SPRING, PRESENT DAY — YES, IT REALLY DID HAPPEN

PRESTON SAT BACK AND looked around him. The rush of hungry, late-night diners had long cleared out since he and Josh had arrived after the Metropolitan House concert. Looking at his watch, Preston realized that the early breakfast crowd would soon be surfacing in the city that never sleeps. He had been talking for almost five hours and couldn't believe how the memories and emotions from that two month season six years ago came flooding back to him. Josh had listened intently for the duration and was now sitting back in his chair staring at

Preston without saying a word. He motioned to the waitress for yet another coffee refill, and he took the last bite of a huge piece of chocolate cake.

"Do you realize how unbelievably amazing … I mean, it's the kind of story that makes a best seller!" Josh said.

"So, are you saying that you liked my story?" Preston asked, trying not to laugh.

"Are you kidding me? Dude, I'm completely blown away!" exclaimed Josh.

"I can see that," Preston said with a laugh.

"No, really. This is something you need to share with the world."

"Maybe," Preston said.

"I'm telling you—it's life-changing. I know it's changed me."

"I'll think about it. To be honest, it's never really crossed my mind."

"Knowing you today, I couldn't imagine you not being athletic as well as a musical prodigy.

"Well, until the end of fifth grade, I was hopeless on the field. It was Ella's Random Act of Kindness that opened this door for me. She helped me make the connection to my music and that's all it took … well, and a whole lot of practice!"

"Now I get it. Ella gave you the note that I found in your case the night of the performance." Josh sat up taller in his chair.

"Actually, that's not when she gave me the note."

"Okay. Hmm … oh, yeah, it was on the day of the kickball tournament, right?

"Nope."

"Then what am I missing?" Josh asked with a hint of frustration.

"You're not missing anything. I didn't share the part when she gave me the note."

"Huh, there's more?" Josh asked, adding sugar and cream to the coffee the waitress poured into his mug.

"Just the fifth grade moving up speech."

"The speech?"

"Yes. Mrs. Grant asked me to share what I learned during my short time at Fern Creek Elementary."

"Okay, go ahead. I'm listening."

"Really?" Preston asked, looking again at his watch.

"You can't stop now. I need to hear the rest. Go on!"

"I guess I can give you the gist," Preston

answered, trying to avoid yawning.

"I'll take it. Wait ... waitress!" Josh waved his hands in the air until he had the waitress's attention. "I'm going to need another piece of chocolate cake, please. Okay, Preston, continue!"

"It was the Thursday night after the concert. The school had invited the fifth grade parents for awards and a moving up ceremony. Mrs. Grant and all the fifth grade teachers passed out awards. I received the Academic Award as I managed to score very well on all the assessments."

"It figures! Go on." Josh said sarcastically.

"Then Mrs. Grant introduced me, and I walked up to the podium. Ella knew I was nervous about sharing my story, so she handed me the note just before I was called up by Mrs. Grant. After reading it, I shoved it in my pocket."

"So, how did it get in your cello case?" Josh asked.

"When I got home that evening, I took it out of my pocket and was going to throw it away, but then I started to think about how much that note meant to me, so I decided to put it in a safe place. Since we were moving, I thought the safest place would be in my cello case. With all the changes in my life, I just never took it out again."

"Glad I found it then! Okay, now let's hear the speech, dude! I'm about to lose my third wind and gain five pounds from all this chocolate cake!"

"I can't remember the speech," Preston said, trying to wrap up the evening.

"Why not?" Josh asked, not willing to let Preston off the hook.

"Because it was something my family and I worked on together. We wrote each paragraph on an index card, all of which are long gone," Preston added.

"Here's an idea—since the story is fresh on your mind, recite what you would say if Mrs. Grant asked you to speak tonight to that very same group of people. Okay, are you ready?"

"I guess," Preston paused, took a deep breath. "Here's goes nothing ...

"Good evening parents, teachers, administration, and classmates. I've been asked to share some things that I have learned since I arrived at Fern Creek Elementary approximately eight weeks ago. My life, as I knew it, came to a sudden stop. I suddenly found myself in a new state, home, and school. To top that, I was given a new identity and look. In fact, I didn't even recognize the face staring back at me in the mirror. I was scared and worried about my dad and our family's future. And I was also completely petrified of participating in the fifth grade kickball tournament.

You see, even though I could play the cello in front of thousands of people without breaking a sweat, I was hopeless in the athletic department. At my old school, I never had to worry about sports. I had the option of speed walking for PE. On that first day of kickball, I tried to get out of playing, but all of my efforts fell on deaf ears. Fear and nerves caused me to faint. My fainting opened the door for bullying, and I was not sure I could survive this new life.

But all that changed with the power of one word—kindness. Kindness came to my rescue in a big way. Thanks to the RAK Initiative,

Ella, along with Thomas and Blake, opened a whole new world for me. They didn't let my fear determine my future. They empowered me to face fear head-on and that led me to face my other fears and conquer them too.

I have called my time as R.J. my synthetic life, but in all honesty, it has been a time when life was very real. I have learned so much from my friends and Mr. Bailey. The biggest lesson I learned is not to let fear win.

We are not exempt from fear because we have talents. Fear visits everyone, no matter the background or status. It's our responsibility to keep kindness alive because for many people, people like me, it makes the biggest difference confronting that fear.

Thank you to all my classmates, especially Trail Blazers Andy, Jennilee, and Sophie, and a special thank you to Mr. Bailey for not only being a phenomenal teacher but a true believer in the power of kindness. You will never be forgotten.

When musicians reach a fermata or grand pause, they must wait for the conductor before continuing. There is no sound or movement. In a way, my life as R.J. has been a grand pause—a waiting—only my grand pause has had plenty of movement and action! It has been a time to grow as a person. It has been a time for me to appreciate my family and hold on to hope. It has been a time to make new friends and learn the power of kindness. Thank you for making my life in the grand pause so amazing!"

"Bravo! Bravo! That was absolutely inspiring," Josh said, rising from his chair.

"Sit down, Josh. You're embarrassing me!"

"I'm only standing up because I need to use the restroom!" joked Josh.

"You're such a goofball!" Preston said, shaking his head.

"Watch it, kid! I'm your ride back to your hotel," said Josh. "One more question."

"Go ahead," said Preston.

"What was Uncle Seth's big announcement?" asked Josh.

"Ha! I knew you were going to ask. Uncle Seth's big announcement was his engagement to Aunt Megan. They were married six months later, and I was Uncle Seth's best man. By the way, Aunt Megan is due to have twins in less than two weeks, and Uncle Seth is so hyped!"

"Very cool! You're going to be a cousin!" Josh said, signing the receipt the waitress delivered.

"Yeah, I hadn't thought about that. I wonder if they'll be anything like me," Preston said.

"The world could use a few more people like you, my friend," he said, patting Preston on the back.

Josh and Preston put on their coats and walked out of the diner. A hint of daylight was beginning to appear in the eastern sky. It had been a long night, but a good night. Josh had been a good listener, and Preston had no idea how impactful his story had been for Josh that evening in April. Preston only knew how grateful he was to have experienced life as R.J. Baker, a student with good friends in Mr. Bailey's fifth grade class at Fern Creek Elementary.

ABOUT THE AUTHOR

AN ELEMENTARY EDUCATOR since 1989, Frank Saraco now gives his imagination, coupled with his experience, a home within the pages of books. Frank masterfully connects words across various genres to capture curiosity and ignite the creativity inherent in all children. His books are filled with rich vocabulary and transition well from pleasurable reading to classroom instruction.

This is Frank's fifth book. Please visit *www.franksaraco.com* to see his other children's books.

And if you have a minute, he'd very much appreciate if you would leave a book review wherever you purchased this book. Reviews help books get found! Thank you!

CPSIA information can be obtained
at www.ICGtesting.com
Printed in the USA
BVHW030813140619
551035BV00003B/5/P